It's a Game of Chase

ISBN: 978-1-7349822-4-4 (Paperback)
ISBN: 978-1-7349822-8-2 (Hardcover)
ISBN: 978-1-7349822-9-9 (Ebook)

This book is a work of fiction. Names, characters, places, and incidents are either the product of the author's imagination or are used fictitiously, and any resemblance to actual persons, living or dead, business establishment, event or locales is entirely coincidental.

Printed in the United States of America.
First printing edition 2020.

Worlds Unknown Publishers
2515 E Thomas Rd,
Ste 16 -1061
Phoenix, AZ 85016-7946

www.wupubs.com

It's a Game of Chase

Maria Wanjiru Ngoda

Worlds Unknown Publishers

CHAPTER ONE

Groundnut Boy

RUTHIE ARRIVED HOME IN THE evening just before dark. She looked at her watch as she headed for the fridge for some cold juice. She wondered whether her life would ever become more interesting. Ruthie sat in the living room and went over her social media. Her online friends had very interesting lives, meeting up after work for cocktails and going out. She wished her life was half as interesting. She barely had a social life. The only time she interacted with people was when she was at work or at the Christian meetings, which she had started going to at the suggestion of their house help. Every day, she went up to her room and stayed there. She really missed her University life; at least there she had her friend, Betty. They did all kinds of crazy things together. She called her for a catch up, but Betty didn't pick up the phone. She lay lazily on her bed until her mother called her for dinner.

"How was your day?" her mother asked her. They were at the dining table with her father and her two younger twin sisters.

"It was okay, same old. You?"

"You know you need to have a social life Ruthie. I worry about you sometimes."

"Well, when I go to church to 'socialize,' you all act as if I have joined a cult. I really feel liberated when I go there."

"You know it's not the same thing, we just- anyway, your brothers will be here soon."

"Ever since they started working in town, they are always here. I think they're old enough to get their own apartments," she responded grumpily as she stood up and took some water and a banana and headed off to her room.

Her family shared glances.

"What's up with her? Did I say something wrong?"

"She's been like that lately. I think she misses the city life," her sister Amina responded.

"Good thing school opens soon, she will soon get her freedom," said her dad as they continued with their dinner. They understood when she needed her space and often left her to deal with it on her own unless it was something harmful or serious.

Ruthie tossed and turned in her bed. She pushed one leg out of the blanket but she was still restless. She sighed heavily as she retrieved her phone from under her double pillows to check the time. Ruthie pressed the on button and squinted at the sudden flash of light in her eyes. It was only six minutes to midnight. She pressed the power button and tried to close her eyes but her mind was as awake as ever.

"My God! What did I do to deserve all this insomnia? *Aaaaaarrrgh!*" She groaned into her pillow and gave it a frustrated punch. Suddenly, she remembered a sermon by her friend Mirembe from the Young Interdenominational Ladies Ministry, a fellowship she had joined in her first year in the university.

"Sometimes when you cannot sleep, God has kept you awake for a reason. It is His quiet time with you. You will seek sleep and you won't find it until you finish fellowship with Him. Only then will you find the sleep you so well desire."

Christianity had been one of her coping mechanisms in her depression. She had gone through extreme bullying in high school; it sank her into depression and gave her nightmares and even made her feel socially awkward. Her father, Mr. Chuma, was a well-known retired judge. He was a strict no-nonsense type of man and always had a clean record. Their local town members were torn between admiring his stature and feeling jealous of him and his family. They lived at the heart of the Rift Valley province in Kenya in a town called Nakuru.

During his time as a judge, her father had made a ruling against a local tea factory, leading to its closure. Many locals had lost their jobs as a result and the town's economy had really tanked. Nobody dared point a finger towards him. He thought that it was all okay after, but boy was he wrong.

When Ruthie had reached the seventh grade, she was taken to a boarding school nearby; it was a great school that recorded high grades and was known for its attention to discipline. She was naturally quiet and kept to herself most of the time. The other students treated her differently and she had a problem making friends but was hopeful that with time everything would be okay. One evening, she went to her dorm room and found pieces of her bucket and basin on her bed. She picked up the pieces but when she sat down to contemplate what had happened, she found that her bed was wet. The students had poured all her stored water on her bedding.

She cried quietly, then reported to the matron what had happened. She was then given an extra set of beddings and the students were summoned and reprimanded. The next evening, when she went in for her evening prep, she found her locker was broken into and all her books torn. There was a warning carved with a nail on her assigned desk reading, "leave this school, or else!" She was so scared that she ran back to her dormitory and explained what had happened to the matron. They spent some time in the matron's cubicle as she took some warm milk. Then she left for her dorm room.

"Aaaaaah!" she screamed loudly as she sank on her knees, hands on her face.

"What's wrong, Ruthie?" The matron went rushing to her room. She just pointed on her bed. It was full of mud and smelt awful, like cow dung.

The matron shook her head in sadness. "I'm so sorry Ruthie. This is not your fault."

"Then whose is it? Why would they do this to me?" she sobbed bitterly. Then they heard some chaos outside.

"Yes! Set them all on fire! In fact, let's go for her box!" one girl shouted.

The matron quickly took Ruthie to her private room and locked her in. Students took her box of personal items and started throwing her things in the fire.

"Please stop! Why are you doing this to her? Stop this at once!" shouted the matron.

"You know why, mattie. Her father cost all of our parents their jobs! Your husband was also a victim. Why should we share this space with her? They should go educate themselves elsewhere!" the ring leader shouted as the rest of the students agreed. Some were pitiful while the rest just enjoyed the scene.

"This is not her fault, please let's just be reasonable, we can always address the situation in a better manner," pleaded the matron as she tried to calm the mob down.

"Hell no! She should also know how it feels like, to have something, then have someone take it all away."

"In fact, we are coming for that long hair of hers if she dares sleep in her bed tonight!" shouted another student. Ruthie could hear the chaos from inside the Matron's room and she broke down in tears. She was so scared.

The matron went and alerted the deputy head master who then called Ruthie's parents to take her away. It was dangerous for her to be in the school any longer. Nobody was in a position to contain the students at that moment. Her parents wanted to sue the school, but Ruthie was against it. Her mother, Pamela, was a senior advocate and a Human Rights activist. She was also fierce and rarely lost her cases. Pamela had received several awards and recognition because of her work andwas also the model wife and mother. Mrs. Chuma often gave to charity and did community outreach on women and children rights. It was the courts that had brought them to the position they were in. Some of their friends also warned them against ifiling a suit against the schoolas it was the best Provincial school and it would cause them more problems if they wanted to continue living in the area. They opted for an out-of-court settlement where the school had to put in strict rules against bullying and have at least two hours per week of counselling on bullying for both pupils and teachers in exchange for Ruthie's parents not suing the school.

It was at this time that they moved to Legacy Estate, a well-guarded and gated estate at the outskirts of Nakuru at the heart of the Rift valley province of Kenya. Nobody entered the estate without a pass from the residents. Each compound was well protected from each other and the residents often kept to themselves. Mr. Chuma had two guard dogs and electric wire around the perimeter of his property.

On the plus side, the compound was big, spacious, and beautiful. They did some great landscaping on their property as well. There was an outdoor pool and a basketball court. The servant's quarters were just a few feet from the kitchen entrance. It was a two-bedroom house where the handyman and his wife, who served as the house help, lived with their two children.

Ruthie was shaken by that experience and had to take a gap year from school, during which time she spent in therapy and home school. After that, she went to a day school nearby in which she also kept to herself and looked forward to taking her final exam.

Since then, she had built a wall around herself and had been determined on being low-key. She rarely used their surname unless she was signing official documents and only socialized with a maximum of three people at a time. She had agoraphobia, she was afraid of being around people, and often experienced panic attacks in crowds.

Their house help had at one point mentioned to her that if she turned to God and gave Him her worries and anxieties and cares, she would be well. This was the genesis of her going for fellowships and church meetings. She preferred small groups, the interdenominational ones. They would talk to each other, meet up for coffee and go for retreats. It was during these meetings that she started talking to one of her neighbors named Stella, who belonged to one of the fellowships. She only went for the Bible Study meetings and prayer meetings as they often comprised of at most ten members.

Ruthie's mind drifted back to the present and she took her phone from under her pillow again and squinted in preparation for the blinding blue light. She went straight to her offline Bible Application and clicked the verse of the day. She found a few verses in the Book of Isaiah that stated that the Lord was doing a new thing in her life. She felt uplifted and decided to plug in her earphones and tune in to her favorite worship playlist. She started singing along in whispers, careful not to wake her parents and siblings in the nearby rooms. She wished she could sneak off to the servant's quarters to hang out with their house girl who had introduced her to Christianity, just for a quick worship session, or at least a talk, but thought against it. It would not be fair to her.

She did not want her family to hear her pray as they would criticize her. They were not atheist, but they did not fancy religion that much. *'Religion is based on one person brainwashing a whole community to do as he pleases and controlling them into making them rich or do as he says,'* her father often said. She wished her family could feel the spiritual awakening she was having. They could never get it if she talked about it. She prayed and cried and worshipped… then drifted off to sleep.

She woke up the next morning late for work and only managed to say a quick *'Good morning Jesus'* in the shower as she believed that even if one couldn't pray, at least acknowledge Him and let Him take you through the day. She hastily glanced in the mirror, applying some lip balm on her wide lips. That was all she was going to put on as makeup. She gathered her relaxed hair into a high bun and hurriedly grabbed her breakfast and packed lunch as she rushed to the bus stop. She had no time to call her local *bodaboda* man to ferry her as she felt he would take his time as always. She luckily got to a *matatu* that had only one space left.

On her way, she received two calls from her supervisor Ms. Mihenzani. She was a young vibrant lady in her early thirties who wore minimum but well-blended makeup, a thin layer of foundation, which one could only notice when she took her phone off her ear where some patches could be seen on the screen, and some lip gloss. She had no children nor the desire for any as she frequently stated. Ms Mihenzani was bold and outspoken and Ruthie really looked up to her. She was very articulate and effortlessly thorough even as she encouraged her staff, interacted with them and shared opportunities for their growth. Mihenzani was wealthy and would occasionally provide tea and lunch for the staff out of her pocket as shecatered the office snacks and occasionally gave the interns and support staff some transport money.

However, Ruthie felt like she did all that to mask her inner sadness. She found her on several occasions in deep thought and often heard her on the phone with someone talking about how depressed she was; she needed a make-over and wanted to give it all up. She had been to rehab twice, once after she came from completing her masters abroad and two years back, according to Janet, who had been working with her from the beginning. She still kept up with the drinking, which really worried Ruthie. She felt like her supervisor needed a friend or something, but she kept all that to herself.

Ms. Mihenzani did everything by the books but once you crossed her clear lines, she would turn into something else. One time the lady at the reception area lied about the balance after being sent for office snacks. She assumed that as always, she would present the receipt and Ms. Mihenzani would put it in her drawer without checking it. She was given an earful of warnings and had to write an official apology letter for embezzlement of office funds and on top of that, had a warning letter attached to her official file. She was a straightforward lady and expected all of her staff to be the same. Her main motto was integrity, just the one word. She insisted that with integrity, everything falls into place.

Ruthie had to profusely apologize to her for the late coming. She knew her supervisor was lenient to her but only within reason.

Ruthie kept her life a mystery and everyone wanted to know what exactly she was all about. She kept her newfound faith to herself and put on a neutral face when in public. She was used to it as her family had slightly different beliefs from her. In the actual sense, she believed that the whole reason people at work, school and surroundings were only lenient, friendly, and interactive with her was due to her mysterious ways. Nobody knew whether she took drugs or alcohol, whether she went out after work, what she did or what her interests were. At one point her supervisor tried to assure her not to worry; if she ever got stranded when she went out for drinks, she was only a phone call away and would come to her rescue. Ruthie widened her eyes at her boss and asked, "Really? You would do that?

"Yes," she replied, "but do not call me when you get arrested with drugs. That is beyond my scope!" She playfully pointed at her as they both laughed.

"Sure thing boss, I sure will keep that in mind," she responded as she picked up signed documents from the desk and walked out.

The afternoon was hot and lazy. Ruthie was slowlygoing through her phone when she received a notification inviting her to a group created by her former classmate who was once her prayer partner in high school. She did not hesitate to join. A meeting was quickly scheduled for the weekend and she knew she had to come up with excuses both at home and work. She turned to Truphosa, her elderly colleague, and asked, "Tomorrow being a Friday, can Ms. M give me the day off? I have something I really need to attend to."

"So, you want a day off tomorrow, huh? Should I clear my schedule as well?" said Sam, the office flirt, as he winked.

"Give her a break, Sam. So, Ruthie, where to? Have you found the one? I hope you've vetted him first before you go for a sleepover. These men who insist you go over even without checking whether you have a job or not are not nice. Can't you go on Saturday?" responded Truphosa. Being married longer than any of their colleagues, she felt the need to spill her nuggets of wisdom at any given point.

"Aaah Phosy, give the girl a break! Let's see the photos first; you have his photos, right?" replied Janet, the office rumormonger, as she stretched her hand towards Ruthie's phone. Janet was the longest-serving employee in the organization and knew everything about everyone, all except for Ruthie's secret life. The one time she had a breakthrough was when she discovered who Ruthie's parents were. They were sitting in the office as she went through her social media when she suddenly gasped.

"Oh my goodness! Do y'all know who Ruthie is? Her dad is the Iron Man himself! Judge Chuma!" she shouted as everyone gasped and Ruthie's face turned a deep shade of red. She was so embarrassed that tears filled her eyes.

"Are you serious? Why didn't you tell us?" Mercy asked, suddenly afraid. "What if we had hurt you or something?" Ruthie could not bear it, she felt so insecure and afraid that it rendered her dumbfounded. She felt this weight fall on her shoulders and tears filled her eyes. Luckily, Ms. Mihenzani walked in at that point.

"What's all the fuss about?" she asked in annoyance.

"Ruthie's father is-" Janet started.

"I know who her father is, so what? This is exactly why I opted to keep it a secret. See how scared the girl is? We always say that this is a safe place for everyone to be comfortable in.

She is just like all of you and if it gets to me that anyone is treating her any differently, it won't end well for you." She paused as she swept the room with a threatening gaze. She then continued, "Janet, that big mouth of yours will land you in problems. Now, get back to work. And Ruthie, I am sorry for all this, please come into my office." Within two days, things simmered down in the office and slowly went back to normal.

Ruthie was extremely annoyed at her imposing co-workers and could not wait to resume her coursework once school started. She was in a good organization, but her colleagues could not keep to themselves. *Who raised these people?* She wondered to herself. She smiled politely at them and their pointless banter as they kept speculating about her. She always watched the time, looking forward to five p.m.

Her mind wandered into the unknown until someone tapped on her desk. Her supervisor was smiling at her. Ruthie had been too engrossed in her thoughts to notice that everyone had scattered.

"Ruthie, are you okay? I was just telling you I am leaving for the day. Do you have anything for me?"

"Oh sorry, okay," Ruthie replied. "No, nothing official. However, can I have Friday off? I will be traveling for the weekend and don't want to travel late at night."

"Aaah, is this finally it? What's his name?" Her supervisor winked at her playfully. "Okay, you can have Friday off, just don't have too much fun and don't forget to come back."

Ruthie slightly blushed and shook her head at her boss. "When that day comes, you will be the first to know, I assure you."

She then turned to her computer as she bid her boss goodbye, shaking her head. The entire staff was eager to please Ms. Mihenzani and do their best work as she had bonuses and motivational presents every half-year for temporary workers and annually for permanent workers. She made her faith, or lack of, very clear. She was an atheist and would encourage any member who felt the need to pray before the meeting to do so at their own will, but only one person per meeting. Never once did Ruthie offer to pray despite her strong faith. She would rather pray in her closet in her office rather than expose herself to what she was recovering from, a cocktail of different kinds of religious beliefs.

Ruthie had experienced nearly three phases of salvation and she felt like they all flopped on her. Her life was overturned several times and she would find herself at the drawing board every single time. She felt like she needed to hit the restart button of her life more often than she would like and felt so confused most of the time. She felt trapped in a world where everyone had a code and she somehow somewhere lost hers. Everyone was living life, strongly, passionately, and with purpose. Her? She just winged it. She would wake up and try to make sense of things, to be in control of her life, but life just seemed to happen no matter what choices she made. She thought herself too weak, too clueless, and even stupid. Every time she would make poor life choices as per her standards-well, standards set by people she thought had the manual for life- she would beat herself up thoroughly and send herself to a place she called BRB, "below rock bottom."

She would curl and sleep there, enjoying the depression for a while as she waited for the next wakeup call. Each time she would go into that phase, she would do all kinds of sinful things with an excuse of finding herself. She would make multiple excuses but eventually decide it was time to wake up. The awakenings were usually accompanied by drastic life events such as sickness, examinations, or craving for a miracle in an area of her life; all this seemed to keep the ball rolling in her life.

Friday evening came, having wasted her entire day off and she was seated in the *matatu* reading a book on her phone when a young man in his mid to late twenties entered. Once he sets his eyes on her, he froze. He gave Ruthie a keen look and assessed her visible features as if looking for something, and proceeded to sit next to her, then moved one seat away so that there was one seat between them. Ruthie found this behavior odd but was thankful that he moved away, as she was keen not to converse with anyone on this journey. Besides, she hated the men who insisted on talking in public vehicles. She felt someone staring at the side of her face and turned abruptly to look at him. She had these curious, wide, piercing dark brown eyes. Once their eyes locked, his heart skipped a beat.

"Hi," Ruthie greeted.

"Uh, hey, hi." He cleared his throat nervously and looked straight ahead. The driver then decided it was time and they had to depart despite the extra empty seat next to Ruthie. The driver asked for fare and Ruthie turned to her seatmate that smelled like trouble and asked him what he was told the fare was, as she had been conned before. When the driver took hers, her seatmate stretched out his arm to give his fare, yet the driver failed to notice it and shut the car door. He put the money back in his pocket and smiled. He then took out ground nuts from his pockets and started eating them.

How uncouth and unfair is this guy? How dare he?! Ruthie thought to herself and promised herself that she would not engage with him at all. *This is just trouble,* she thinks, plus she had experience with these kinds of people. He was a screaming red flag and she knew this would end in tears, waterfalls of tears. While she was busy judging her seatmate, and hoping for the angels to create a hedge of protection from the temptation, she could feel his blatant stares. She decided to wear her earphones and zone out. Then, she drifted off to sleep.

Ruthie was woken up by a loud car horn. She looked out and it was dark. Looking at the time, it was nine thirty p.m. She thought about the events of the day. She had received a call from her neighbor Stella, requesting to visit some campsites in the next town, Gilgil, where they would go with some of their neighborhood friends for a retreat. She told her friend that she had Friday off but she would be travelling to Nairobi for a meeting. Her friend convinced her that they would go in the morning and she would have plenty of time in the afternoon to travel as it was a three-hour drive. She took out her phone and went over the pictures they had taken of the campsites and themselves in the wild. She smiled as she watched one where they had to cross a river ferried by a donkey cart.

"We have to go back, Ruthie. Could that campsite be any better than the ones we have seen?" Stella had asked in fear.

"Don't be a chicken Stella, it's just a river. I've heard good things about that place, plus crossing the river will have will be a much better adventure for us. See how far we have walked."

"Is there another way around it? Or a much better means? Do we have to use the donkey?" she asked the man who was offering them his best, less bloody donkey to ferry them across.

"No there is no other way; even white tourists use these donkeys," he responded trying to market his services.

"Alright, I will go first. Help me up," said Ruthie as she went towards the donkey, deaf to Stella's protests. She was ferried across the river, her heart in her throat, but she couldn't show her fear so as not to scare Stella further. She quickly alighted the beast of burden when she got to dry land and watched as the man took the donkey back to carry Stella.

"See, I'm still alive and in one piece. Hurry up, we don't have all day!" she shouted at her friend.

"No," she said taking off her shoes and folding up her trousers, "I will go across by myself. I'm not boarding that thing."

"Okay then, just get ready for some snakes and worms and other slimy animals in the river. I've tried my best," said the man with the donkey, as he turned to go sit under the shade waiting for other customers.

"Wait! Stop! Are you serious? Okay, please go slow and be very careful," said Stella with balancing tears in her eyes. She held onto the man so tightly and kept screaming as the donkey swayed away. Ruthie, on the other hand, was laughing so hard her sides ached. She held her stomach and tears flowed down her cheeks, unable to control herself. She raised her eyes to look at Stella as she caught her breath and unfortunately caught a glimpse of her violently vibrating top due to her erratic heartbeat. Ruthie felt a fresh wave of laughter and burst out again. She shut her eyes and started controlled breathing exercises as she attempted to control her laughter, ease her stomach pains, and concentrate on not peeing her pants. She looked away for composure until the donkey crossed over with her precious cargo. Stella shakily alighted, assisted by two men, as Ruthie recorded it amidst Stella's protests. She now had one over Stella. She was smiling fondly at her memories when she felt someone tap her shoulder.

"Sorry to interrupt your fantasy, but what's the time?" Ruthie's seatmate asked, awakening her from her daydream. Ruthie internally rolled her eyes, did some safe cussing, then responded with the time, putting on the facade she always put when talking to strangers with a slight smile. She clicked her tongue with annoyance inwardly at his use of 'fantasy,' and felt offended. This judgmental guy was just jumping to conclusions. Ruthie then wondered why she hated this stranger with all this passion. Even how he eats groundnuts just annoyed her. *Does he need that many groundnuts? Why exactly? Didn't he eat before coming here?* Ruthie then realized that she was being judgmental and too critical of a total stranger who had absolutely nothing to do with her. She decided to keep reading her book on her phone. She could not concentrate on a simple interesting novel; her mind kept thinking how annoying this groundnut boy was. He really got under her skin.

Ruthie enjoyed making these trips to the city, be it going to school, meeting up with friends, or most excitingly her recent Christian missions. She started thinking of her travel escapades and the different men she had met in these escapades. She remembered meeting this upcoming artiste called Imani as she was travelling to school for the first semester of her third year in the university. She had sat next to him at the mid-section of the shuttle.

"Hi, do you mind if I put my guitar here? I chose this seat because of the room," he started.

"Sure, no problem. Are you a musician?" Ruthie responded.

"Ha-ha, not really, but I perform music during events. I write my own music, but you know this country. I'm Imani by the way, and you are?" he asked.

"Oh, I'm Ruthie. Nice to meet you. What do you mean by this country? Don't you need to meet up with a producer and start making your music?"

"It's not that easy. You need a renowned producer to make your music heard. They are too expensive and they often massacre your music. I do a different kind of music and have my own style that they just don't get," he responded. Ruthie decided not to prompt him further on the topic as she felt like he would lose it. She felt like it was opening some wounds that she would not be able to handle.

"So where are you headed?" she asked instead.

"There is a wedding coming up and I was hooked up with the gig. I will be the guitar player there and will also serenade the bride as she walks in. Lucky girl, huh?" he said. Ruthie smiled as they chatted along.

She learnt that Imani was so good in almost all musical instruments, and had an amazing voice. He sent her some of his music on the way and she listened to them on her earphones to judge for herself. It was good music, but Ruthie preferred a deeper voice. Ruthie had been interested in music since she was young. Imani made her explore her musical taste and found joy in music she previously paid no attention towards. Make no mistake, music really spoke to her body, mind, and soul. She felt goosebumps whenever she felt a certain beat or vocal or tune. She felt her brain come alive whenever she heard a certain background layer of voices and could feel the beats in her pulse and each time she heard music, especially from her favorite artistes, she could tell the difference in style or the uniqueness in each line. Like snowflakes, each was beautifully different. She had once tried her hand in music by singing, writing music, and even playing certain instruments like the *kayamba* when she was young, then the tambourine, and harmonica and then graduated to the keyboard. Now, her interest was the guitar.

She thought she had found her muse that would help her be more in touch with her musical side and make it grow into something. All she had been doing was acquiring new interests then dropping them because she would either lack the motivation to do it or simply get bored. Other times, she would be ashamed of showcasing her talents amongst her friends, due to fear of being ridiculed.

She had then found herself engaging Imani so much, but she quickly lost interest. He was too sentimental, touchy-feely, and a bit too feminine for Ruthie's liking. He had a weird sense of style, ripped skinny jeans, long combed-out hair, long nails, and ironic t-shirts. He kept saying how deep he was, how deep some artistes are, deep talkers, deep texting, it soon grew old. Besides the mix tapes and new music he kept sharing with her, and the acoustic guitar he carried everywhere unnecessarily, there really was nothing much about him. Frankly, even the music started growing old. Some of the music he called "deep" soon started making absolutely no sense to Ruthie. He became nagging and insecure despite Ruthie making it clear that she had no interest in dating and they were only friends. She then decided it was time for mister "deep-clingy" to go. She attempted blocking him on all platforms but somehow, he kept coming back. He would even send friends to tell her that he was not okay and would like an audience for her to explain why she was ghosting him. One time, he even threatened to stop his music career for her, but Ruthie threatened to report him to the authorities for being a stalker; this was harassment. Imani was the man that had made her stop talking to these travelling weirdoes who insisted on emotional attachment on first sight.

She then felt some unrest in the vehicle; passengers were craning their necks. She paused her music and unplugged her earphones. "Hey! Let me alight here! Where are you taking us?" they demanded. She craned her neck and saw the driver keep going past Odeon Cinema, her normal stop, then tea room, the final bus stop she was aware of and then turned a corner so fast that the women in the vehicle started screaming and the men were hurling insults and threats towards the driver. He then came to an abrupt stop. Ruthie was saying her prayers and even switched to tongues inside her head. The groundnut boy had scooted over to her side by the time the *matatu* stopped and as soon as Ruthie opened her eyes, she found the bemused young man staring at her again. Really, how uncouth can one be?

She then heard the driver hurriedly apologize, partly blaming the passengers for not listening when he announced where he would drop them. He even told the passengers to behave like the city dwellers they appeared to be. Everyone, including Ruthie, clicked their tongue in annoyance as they alighted the *matatu* and no one thought to thank the driver. She looked at her watch and it was 10pm. How was she going to reach uptown on her own?

"Hey again, stranger. You look stranded. Do you know where we are?" God! The nerve on this man!

She sighed and looked at the man, "Yes, this inconsiderate bastard just dropped us off at *Nyamakima* despite the time. And where in *Nyamakima* does he choose? The dingiest of backstreets that ever existed." That was the last stage at the very edge of Nairobi city.

"Bastard?" He sucked some air through his front teeth and cringed. "You don't seem like one to cuss." He grinned cheekily at her. Ruthie could not resist rolling her eyes for the umpteenth time since she met this groundnut boy. *Why is he so interested?* Yes, she needed someone to walk with in this darkness for protection purposes, but then again, she could easily pick any of the passengers. She looked around noticing everyone hurriedly scattering into pairs. She then decided she had no choice but walk with Mr. Groundnuts for her own safety.

"Okay fine, I'm Ruthie. You are?"

He smiled widely and responded, "You can call me Ethan." He started walking and Ruthie tried hard to catch up. He was really tall but looked a bit too weak to fight off any thugs in case of an attack. His face looked thuggish, though, so Ruthie gave him the benefit of doubt. Well not so thuggish, but tough. He was around six feet tall, had a goatee just like Ruthie loved, was lean, and took long bouncy strides. She found his walking strides quite amusing. He had short hair with a small neat cut on the left side just before the fade and the top front part of his hair was wavy. Ruthie wondered whether he went to the salon to achieve that look or whether barber shops offered the services.

"So, are you going to follow me until we arrive at the bus stop or are you going to walk with me? These streets are not safe. I won't bite, promise." Something about this man's smile made Ruthie cringe inwardly. It looked more of a smirk than a smile as it was only one-sided and his eyes held a cheeky glance while he "smiled." She leapt forward and caught up with him, struggling to keep up with his pace. He had this urgent sprint in his walk that made Ruthie almost give up on walking with him.

"What do you do?" Ruthie asked.

"Right now, I am interning at a firm here in town. I am a final-year student at the university, majoring in architecture and minoring in interior design. I know, it's just an interest for me, and I am not gay. I have nothing against that life choice but I just feel the need to say that," he broke off and stopped to look at Ruthie who was looking back at him, curiosity in her eyes.

"Relax," she responded finally breaking the silence. "I don't judge either, I think it is pretty cool to be interested in something perceived feminine. It's pretty bold too for a traditional African man like you. Also, I wouldn't have judged you even if you were gay." She giggled as she said the last part.

"What exactly does that mean? "Traditional African man like myself?" Aren't you already judging me? What is traditional typical African about me? And I still insist I'm as straight as an arrow- straighter even."

"Who protesteth too much?" Ruthie said in a sing-song voice as she smiled at how she was getting under his skin. She enjoyed every bit of how uncomfortable he was. She could have sworn she even saw a thick vein pop on his forehead then disappear as something flashed in his eyes, quickly covered by the façade he had been trying to keep up. "I'm just messing with you, calm down. Anyway, I will be doing my final year in communication and public relations this September. I am also interning at a firm out of town."

"Why are you so trusting? What if I am a serial killer, or a human trafficker?"

They had arrived at the town center and were strolling towards nowhere in particular. Ruthie looked at him calmly and responded, "What are the chances that two serial killers found each other?" They both laughed as they walked on.

"Do you mind having a drink with me? It's still early and we seem like we have one thing in common," he said, winking at her. Ruthie hesitated a bit, remembering how she had vowed not to be sucked into this kind of life again.

"Actually, I quit drinking, plus I have a long way to go. But it was nice meeting you. Where are you getting your bus or whatever?"

He took out his phone and handed it to her. "At least give me your number. We could have coffee sometime as we discuss how to grow our criminal empire." Ruthie gave him her number but failed to even laugh at his insensitive, satanic, unprincipled offer.

"You know a joke is only said once, unless you really are that kind of person, I don't know why you should drag me into your evil habits."

"Sorry, what?"

"I am saved; I thought you should know."

Ethan looked at her for a bit and smirked.

"So, my bus, "or whatever," is there. Should I escort you to yours or will the Holy Spirit escort you?" Ruthie had had enough of this man. She felt like taking his phone and deleting her number from it. He was too much; she even felt tears well up in her eyes as something stuck in her throat.

"Cat got your tongue? Look, I was just being friendly Ruthie, you just seem so uptight and I felt like you need to let loose. I am sorry if I offended you but there is no need to treat me like a stranger. I will take you to your bus stop." Ruthie finally composed herself and a fresh wave of anger and annoyance swept through her.

"Look here, groundnut boy. You don't know me, I don't know you, and frankly I find you so damn annoying; you have been getting on my nerves ever since I set my eyes on you! You are uncouth and imposing, horrible, inconsiderate and just too much. And just so you know, nobody eats that much groundnuts, you risk loose bowels and I am glad I don't live with you. This is my bus stop, so please don't sit next to me." She rolled her eyes and clicked her tongue in annoyance as she walked towards the bus. It was nearly empty. She got in and found a seat near the window and sat. Ethan was left dumbfounded on the streets trying to internalize what this strange girl had said. He tried to replay the events prior to the outburst and the more he thought about it, the more confused he got. He then rushed towards the bus and found that nobody had sat next to her yet. Ruthie saw him, rolled her eyes, and sneered at him as she dug around in her bag for earphones and her phone. Ethan went next to her and sat, looking at her as if he was searching for something.

"First of all, *groundnut boy*? Really?" he started, looking deep in her brown eyes. Her lips tagged at the corner. "No, don't talk. You don't just insult someone in the streets and expect them to just leave it at that. Did you want some?"

Ruthie's eyes grew wide in bewilderment, "What?"

"I meant, do you want some groundnuts? Not so saved after all, huh?" he grinned as he said the last part almost inaudibly, but Ruthie had heard him.

"Why do you hate me so much when you don't know me? From the first time you set your eyes on me? Crush alert!" he said. "Maybe you really do like me and are afraid, or someone hurt you recently and had my awesome vibe, or…"

"Please just shut up! When I woke up this morning, everything was fine. My life lately has been amazing and awesome, and I have been happy and content with how my life has been until I met you. That's it. In fact, I would *never* in a million years be in a relationship with, or even like someone like you. So to answer your question, I just hate you as a person and I do not need your groundnuts, I am never going to need your groundnuts, and if we could get home in silence, I will be grateful." She then looked straight on. *Why am I this mad?* She wondered. This man has been nothing but kind to her. Maybe he was a bit presumptuous and uncouth, overbearing and boundary-challenged but even worse, he made her cuss, hate, and even sin in her mind.

"You have a lot of pent-up energy that needs to be released, Ruthie. I am just trying to make a new friend here. You know I also got intrigued by you when I saw you. To be honest, I was drawn to you because you look like someone really dear to me. I am sorry for offending you and I will get out of your hair now." Ruthie grabbed his arm as he stood up to switch seats. She felt guilty for lashing out at him for no reason and suddenly touched his wrist hoping that he would at least consider her apology.

"Okay, maybe I overreacted. I am also sorry. What I did was uncalled for. Yes, I am a saved Christian and yes, I can make new friends, no matter their consumption of nuts," she said, smiling at him.

Ethan took a packet of unopened mixed nuts from his trench coat and handed them to her. "Truce?"

She took them, smiling. "I have nothing against them by the way, I just think you eat way too much."

She opened the packet after sanitizing her hands and popped multiple into her mouth as Ethan looked at her, clearly amused. "Need some yoghurt to wash that down?" he asked, laughing. Ruthie playfully smacked his hand and continued munching away. She took some water from her bag as the bus finally filled up and started moving. "So where do you stay? Or rather, where are you going?" Ethan asked.

"I stay near the airstrip at mother Theresa Court- well my aunt stays there and I will be going to her place today. Hopefully I will find someone awake to let me in because it is getting really late and this bus is really slow. You?" she answered, taking another sip off water, worry suddenly registering on her face.

"I just moved in to the next court, Tausi. I guess it seems that we were destined to find each other, huh?"

"You know, it's things like that that really make me feel like pushing you off your seat. I used to believe in life and easy things: destiny, love, you know, but you, Ethan, seem like the type that eats life with a big spoon. You sway through life, things are easy, you have fun, and all with no real consequences since things just work out for you, you didn't even pay the fare to get here. You can easily fool people with your charm and are not ashamed to show strangers like me, a beautiful girl who rudely blew you off, your outrageous views and outlook in life. I really don't hate you, I just, I don't know…"

Ethan had been quiet this whole time listening to her. She had not even noticed that during her rant the conductor had already asked for their fare and he paid for the both of them. He wanted to respond when she started at it again, "You know, my life has been both easy and hard, and I have not dated anyone for such a long time and I keep changing my life to see the different versions of myself that I can be, safely, and just live life the correct way as I enjoy people like you.

"Maybe that's what has made me angry, I envy how you live life so easily and that it's working out well for you."

Ethan burst out laughing for a while as he held his sides. By the time he was done, there were tears in his eyes. Ruthie just stared at him. *How could he laugh at my life crisis?* She regretted even asking him to stay.

Ethan finally composed himself and looked at her, compassion filling his eyes. "Ruthie look, we literally just met, literally! All you know about me is based on what I have told you in less than an hour and the rest of it you either judged me or assumed. Also, you have not paid your fare so…" He gestured with his arms as he smiled fondly at her and added, "You seem really nice and I would like to know you more, even just as friends and maybe we can figure out this whole perfect life thing together?" He had her.

Ruthie felt a weight lift off her chest- well, maybe two was more accurate. They made an ice cream date and started talking about other things as they laughed.

Ruthie could not believe she had let this man charm his way into her life, but he was not so bad as a friend. She wondered who this mystery twin of hers was and pushed it at the back of her mind to ask during their date.

Finally, the bus came to their stop and they alighted, strolling slowly towards their dusty path. The sky was clear that night and calm. It was like a romantic walk under a dark blue blanket, frosted with sparkling diamonds and a bright yellow light shining on their path. They inhaled the cool wind into their lungs as it refreshed their souls. Everything was just right. They got so engrossed in their comfortable stroll and it was like the whole world stopped and gave them time to forget everything and enjoy the now. Ruthie then realized that it was getting late and decided to call her aunt, informing her of her arrival. She did not pick up after three calls and two messages. Ethan told her not to worry, he would keep her company until she responded. They walked up to the gate and tried knocking with no success.

"I, um, promise not to do anything at all, but feed and keep you company," he said counting his fingers as he looked up. "It's getting late and, *uum*, maybe we should go to, eh, eh, ahem, *mmh,* my place. It's a one-bedroom apartment I will take the couch you can have the bed, or whatever makes you comfortable." Ethan offered amid stammers. "I know you are a Christian with principles, and that thing about human trafficking—"

"Ethan, it's really late, we had a long journey. Let me just text my aunt informing her that I slept over at a friend's house in Tausi then we can go. I appreciate your kind offer."

27

CHAPTER TWO

Hell Hath No Fury

ALMOST EVERYONE HAD ALREADY ARRIVED at the prayer conference when Ruthie arrived. She quietly sat in the back as she smiled at her friends. She looked at the person beside her and one seat away was Betty, her partner in crime and author of most of her escapades. Their journey in life had been almost similar except for the fact that Ruthie felt Betty had hers fairly figured out and balanced. She also seemed to call the shots in her life and even others'. Heck, she even managed to change her full name before she was thirteen, according to her stories. I mean, who is given a name by her parents and decides at a tender age that she prefers another one?

Her name originally had been Regina Kawira. She had grown up hating her first name because everyone called Regina had a timid character, and she felt like it did not best describe her. Her parents tried to tell her about the Reginas in their bloodline who were bold and great but she could hear none of it. The last straw was when she went home from school and found that their neighbor's domestic house help was called Regina. As for Kawira, every local television program had a comical cheeky girl by that name. She had recently been transferred to a boarding school in another province and she took advantage of the situation to change her name.

She decided to go to the senior teacher and inform him about the new name and her parents' request to bring in the amended birth certificate which she would use to register for her national exam. She was surprised that he took it lightly, stating that it happened with many students. They often realized that the name they were referred to did not match their birth certificates. So, he would just write a message to her parents to bring in her birth certificate during the academic day.

Her registration had already been submitted to the National Exams Council with her chosen name by the time her parents brought in her birth certificate for confirmation of names. Her parents would have no other choice but to comply. When her parents went for visiting day after the whole name-changing fiasco, they had looked for her for close to an hour with her former name without any success, until finally when she saw her frustrated father and weeping mother, she went and informed them of the new developments. Eventually they had to give in and legally changed the name.

Her new official name now was Betty Kamene. She had taken the second name from her favorite aunty. She fancied her aunty's character and wanted to be just like her when she grew up.

She had managed to change her course after one year by stating that it was not her calling, even after her parents paid her fees and bribed their way into the university since she had not yet attained the legal age for admittance and had not yet acquired her national identity card. She transferred to an International College in the city to study Culinary Arts after she had eventually gotten her national identity card. She chose to get a Bachelor's Degree in Foods and Nutrition and Dietetics as a major and Interior Design as a minor course.

Her parents tried to convince her that she would study her culinary arts as a hobby and receive a certificate only, but she was adamant. That was not all: she even managed to join her new campus politics group during her first year in the university and won as the secretary general of the student union by a landslide. She was a force to reckon with and a go-getter. She always seemed to have everything under control except her love life, sometimes Christian life and, more often than not, she was always misunderstood and therefore made very few female friends.

Betty was Ruthie's goon; whenever she needed ideas on sweet revenge she knew she could always count on Betty. Even when she needed a backsliding buddy, she had a friend in her. They would decide to go out have some drinks, dance the night away, and make some bad decisions or better, drink bottles of wine and watch movies all night. One time, Ruthie had disagreed with her housemate to the extent of physical fighting. Betty, as usual, came to her rescue and as they were in the room discussing on revenge methods, Ruthie suggested drugging her friend and watching her suffer.

"Wait a minute, is she not the one who judged me for smoking marijuana and threatened to report me to the authorities? Well I got something for her." Betty suddenly said, sprinting towards the wardrobe, excitement written all over her face. She fished out her bag and started searching for something. She took out a tiny marijuana bag. "Tadaa!" she said in a singsong voice, her eyes practically glowing with excitement as Ruthie jumped and snatched the bag away from her.

"Oh my goodness Betty! Are you crazy? I told you that is not safe here."

"No girl, hear me out. We could cook dinner as a peace offering then we can add this to the veggies. I will even buy pork. Please? She needs to learn her lesson, let's watch as she freaks out. This is a once-in-a-lifetime chance."

Ruthie gave it a thought and shook her head. "No, I will just move out. She doesn't even fancy pork. Also, what makes you think she would eat our food? We both know that's not how to cook with pot anyway." They argued about it and eventually Ruthie gave in and their plan worked.

They sat on her roommate Karen's bed and ate as they listened to music and sipped their wine. They apologized to each other and soon enough everyone was laughing. Karen never really liked wine, she enjoyed her gin and vodka strictly so she just enjoyed the company until she started feeling breathless. She stripped and went to the balcony freaking out. She complained that she felt dizzy and confused. She wanted to jump from the fourth-floor balcony when Ruthie decided she had had enough fun and dragged her to her bed where she dived and started swimming among the blankets. She did her breast strokes, back stroke and even a butterfly. When she had finally gotten tired, she decided she was at a military base and took the blow drier and started making shooting sounds as she ran around the house, killing villains and fighting off terrorists. Betty was having the time of her life as she recorded all these events on her phone.

Ruthie started getting worried when Karen took in endless amounts of water as if she felt dehydrated. She was tempted to tell Karen about the drugging but she could not. Karen was studying for her law degree and she did not want to risk being sued for whatever crime Betty was busy committing in their house. Suddenly, Karen paused and looked at her friends, suspicious. "Did you guys drug me? Is that why I am acting strangely? Why did you call this bitch here? I'm calling the police on you, I can't believe you guys, I am so dumb, where's my phone?"

She started crying as she looked for her phone. Betty, in her criminal mind, had already hidden it and was now locking the doors with a padlock and taking custody of the keys. "Look Karen," Ruthie started.

Betty butted in quickly, interrupting her. "You are overreacting and we were having a good time. Maybe take a rest. We will talk about this tomorrow, as well about your vampire tendencies, do you remember biting Ruthie's arm? What if she reports you for assault? Just sleep, bitch." Miraculously, this pep talk worked and as soon as she was done speaking, Karen slowly sat on her bed nodding as she quietly sniffed, wiping her tears. She reached for her sweats and t-shirt and put them on. "Good girl, now sleep your sorrows away and next time please think twice before you attack my feeble Ruthie, okay?" Betty patted her head and switched off the lights. They retreated to Ruthie's room laughing their asses off, and that was the most fun they had ever had, at least in Ruthie's books.

She always thought that Ruthie had a split personality, the purest of hearts was the main one, but sometimes she would turn into an extremely evil force to reckon with; the devil sometimes would sit and take notes whenever Ruthie's demons awoke. Not even Betty could contest her in that state, like the time when she created a fake account and got into a side relationship with her own philandering boyfriend Otieno.

She had dated Otieno since she was in high school and to her, he was all she needed. They had the exact age gap she wanted in a husband, he was masculine enough, understanding, and told her fascinating stories about university that inspired her to move to the city. She ran away from home in order to enroll to university. When her parents finally came around, she happily joined the university and dated Otieno for two years. He treated her well at first and they were so in love up until he started acting strange. He would ignore her for days, party for weeks, and even abuse her emotionally. He told her that he was the whole reason she came to the city and nobody loved village girls like her. He killed her self-esteem and her social life. Not even her sisters could make her understand that she was being abused. She contracted sexually transmitted infections and he would get over-the-counter medication for her.

He then started physically abusing her and would shed tears if Ruthie ever threatened to leave him. He would cry and apologize on his knees, promising a new start, but would eventually go back to the animal he was. He was much stronger than her, even though he was a short, plump man. He was only two inches taller than her and for this reason forbade her from wearing high heels as he would seem shorter than her. She got pregnant by him in her second year of college and things got much worse. He would sleep with other women and even bring them to his house in front of Ruthie. She called Betty and she helped her pack her clothes and when the man came and found them packing, he locked all the doors and started crying profusely. It sounded like loud bitter mourning she had heard from the villagers when her grandmother died.

Again, much to Betty's disapproval, she unpacked and even cooked for him. He made a promise to Betty, his unborn child, and Ruthie that he would never ever do anything bad to them again. He even swore, carrying a bible, kneeling down while in tears. He was extremely theatrical. Betty kept reminding Ruthie that she was not married and that she had a right to abort the baby and start living her life. She called Ruthie naïve and brainwashed; Ruthie then decided that she was just jealous and cut her off. Her boyfriend started disappearing again, and this time she decided to take matters into her own hands. She created a fake online dating profile and matched with him. They had a serious relationship and then the demands to meet her became too much that they set a date. He even promised that he had stopped searching and had found the one in her. He was in love.

When the material day came, he lied that he had a trip to the coast and should Ruthie need anything, she should say it then, because there would be no network where he was going so his phone would be off. She pretended that she was unwell and had not even eaten nor showered when he left. She asked for emergency money, knowing well that she needed the transport and salon money to go and meet him. She had tried to call Betty a few times to talk to her about Otieno and apologize, hoping to possibly get her input, but to no avail. She was ten weeks pregnant now, her emotions were running wild, and maintaining these two sides was becoming hard for her. She needed someone to help her.

She had spent night after night crying while flirting with Otieno as another woman and she concluded that she was crazy. He kissed her goodbye and left. Her phone rang and much to her delight it was Betty. She broke down as she explained how she had been and apologized to her. Within the hour, Betty was by her side and encouraged her to go ahead and bust him. He had made reservations for them at a hotel about an hour from the city and it broke Ruthie's heart. They went to the salon and had her hair and nails done, Betty even bought her lipstick and shoes for good luck. Her pregnancy was not showing but her bust and ass were popping in the right manner; she smiled at the reflection in her mirror.

Her phone dinged. It was a text from Otieno, *"Can we talk now? I hope you are on your way, you will find your new phone with me so that I can call you as much as we can and just talk, before you agree to move in with me and officially be my wife. (Smiley face emoji)"* Betty rolled her eyes and almost called him. Ruthie told her to calm down, she had an agreement with the local lady who sold her coastal dishes to talk to him on the phone on occasion in order to maintain the lie. She would pass by before she left and talk, informing him that she had just left.

"You know, at first I was unsure, but now, I am really starting to appreciate this side of you, but what is the end game? After you bust him, what's next? He will still cry and you will forgive him and then enjoy your make-believe honeymoon."

Ruthie continued putting her makeup on and then a bright idea suddenly hit her. "Let's go together, B. I want you to witness my full wrath, he is going to know exactly who I am."

She smiled an evil smile at her own reflection that made Betty shudder...then worry. Betty asked Ruthie whether she should make calls for backup, but Ruthie just smiled and shook her head, adding that she would cater for her transport and any other fee. Betty became so worried that she accepted to follow her for everyone's safety. *"Baby talk to me, are we still on?"* Ruthie confirmed that she was on her way and confirmed the location of the hotel. Then her actual phone rang and it was Cedric calling.

"Our ride is here, girl, let's go."

A puzzled Betty followed along, very worried, and they went towards a maroon Nissan Xtrail. Betty was amused until she saw Ruthie kiss the driver affectionately and get into the co-driver's seat. Betty was worried three times. "Hey, you must be the rock. I'm Cedric, the other rock," he winked at Betty and she could just not hold it anymore.

"First of all, I am Betty, her main and only rock and I hope this was not your brilliant idea. She is very fragile, you know?" Ruthie shouted at them to get in before she bashed both of their heads together. They looked at each other as Cedric raised his hands, shaking his head, indicating that he was in the dark as well. They travelled as they chatted like old friends laughing, singing along to Ruthie's music. She kept making demands which Betty passed off as pregnancy hormones until they reached the hotel. They checked in and went into Ruthie's room in tense silence. She opened a bottle of really expensive whiskey and poured into two glasses, ordering them to drink if they wanted to enjoy the show. She lit up a joint and started smoking; everyone was quiet. She then took the glasses and downed the drinks in a swift move and poured them more. They took the glasses from her hands and she smiled at them. She continued smoking as she kept checking her phone. Finally, she decided to text him stating that she was twenty minutes away and he responded that he was already there, she should go straight to the bar on arrival, and he was ordering food and drinks. She smiled and pulled out a little black dress that really accentuated her figure and started dressing in front of her dumbfounded guests. Nobody was talking.

"Aren't you guys going to change? Betty, touch up that make up and Cedric, off with that sweater. I want the whole world to see that expensive watch, plus it doesn't not go well with those sexy eyes," she winked.

They took shots knowing fully well that they were dealing with a crazy woman and the best they could do was wait and see where she falls so that they could hold her. They gave each other knowing looks as they tried to look their best for their crazy friend. They both knew better than to question her or try anything stupid, so they complied. She put on her red heels and lipstick. She looked stunning. They locked the room and started off to the bar. She stopped at the door and located Otieno, her soon to be ex-boyfriend, then went and sat on the table next to the counter stool, where he was seated. He stared at her, confused at first until the realization dawned on him. He looked so scared and started looking towards the door. She stood and motioned for her friends to stay seated. She strutted like a runway model towards him and pulled up a stool. She then called the waiter and ordered a shot of tequila rose. He cancelled the order and asked for a glass of juice. "Scratch that, I would like a pitcher of long island cocktail for my friends over there and a screwdriver for me," she said, winking at the impressed bartender who then smiled shyly and left when her boyfriend gave him a look.

"What exactly are you trying? Why are you here? What are they doing here and who is that bastard?"

"My darling, that should be the least of your worries. My question is, do you not know where the coast is or where exactly did you say you were going?" He nervously looked towards the entrance for the millionth time and then excused himself to go to the bathroom. Suddenly, her fake phone rang. "He... he... hello?" he stuttered, "Where are you?"

"There has been a change of plans," Ruthie smiled an evil one. "Come back, our drinks are here." Then she hung up. Otieno instantly got sober and felt his bowels go lose, a wave of nausea and dizziness hit him, He went and threw up in the bathroom, then washed his face as he tried to think about the situation. He felt like he was dreaming. He confirmed the numbers again and decided to walk back with fresh anger. He needed a backup plan. How would he twist this? Should he say that he knew all along and since it had been her all along that it was not cheating? He then remembered all the conversations and just got confused and angry; he even felt tears in his eyes.

He walked towards the bar and found her still drinking alone as her friends kept watching her carefully. He got so scared because if Betty had sat in that distance then things were crazy. He passed their table without a word and went straight to his former seat which now felt like hot lava.

"Babe, are you high? Drunk? Why are you here? I think in your condition-"

"Shut up! What condition? Are you supposed to be promising other women marriage in *your* condition? Are you supposed to go out of town for days and even book expensive hotels like this in your condition?"

He knew he was in trouble, never had she ever drank this way in his presence, looked this good, nor talked back to him. He was the alpha dog of the relationship from the onset, who was this woman now? "So Ninah, huh? You really promised her way more than your own baby mamma and girlfriend of three years. Where is my new phone? The food? Are you dumb, now? Don't you dare shed those stupid crocodile tears of yours. They make me sick!" She spat on the bar floor in disgust. She saw Betty trying to get up in her periphery and Ruthie raised her arm to stop her. "You took away three years of my life and you're about to take the rest of it. Who do you think you are?" She looked up at him. He was scared. "I am talking to you Dumbo, what the hell?"

He cleared his thought and responded, "We are Christians and please, baby, baby please, let's take this up to my room, our room please."

"Aaah where there would be *no witnesses?* You have been beating me up behind closed doors, I treat infection after infection, I don't know who I am anymore. I lost everything including my worth, identity, esteem, beauty, and pride. I am here to take it all back." She took a swig of his remaining beer and put it back.

"Ruthie, you don't scare me at all. I can hold you with one arm and bend you over my knee for a good spanking and you won't do shit."

Her eyes turned red in anger and she saw red all over. She took the bottle of beer and broke it on the counter then hit him on the head in one swift move, then started hitting and hitting endlessly. She was kicking punching and throwing. Otieno tried to defend himself and punched her in the stomach; she didn't feel any pain at the moment. She took off her shoe and hit him in the head with it as she slapped and kept punching him all over. Otieno threw a last kick which landed on her abdomen again as Betty let out a scream. Suddenly as she was lunging forward to attack him again, she felt strong arms lift her out as she screamed her lungs out. The last thing she remembered was blood on the counter and her lifeless boyfriend on the ground. She had one heel in her arm as Betty was following with another stained one. She was hysterical.

The next morning, she woke up in a hospital bed, her body aching all over. Betty rushed to her side and told her not to move. She heard Cedric's voice in the distance calling for the nurse.

She tried to talk but her throat was dry. She could not do anything. She was in so much pain that tears started rolling down her face. Betty rubbed her arm as she wiped her face, whispering words of reassurance in her ears. The nurse quickly came and added something in her drip and she felt her eyes grow heavy and her body went limp once more.

When she finally regained her consciousness, she was feeling a bit better. She saw Betty on her side with different clothes sleeping soundly as Cedric was going through his phone. He looked up and rushed to her side.

"You okay there, ninja? How are you feeling today?" Ruthie gestured towards her throat and Cedric brought her a cup of water to sip from. She felt awful and weak.

"Was I dead? When time is it? Where are we? Oh my goodness, did I kill him?" she asked suddenly widening her eyes in fear as tears freely rolled down her cheeks. "I'm so sorry, Cedric, I didn't mean it, am I in a prison hospital? Did you say it was self-defense? I can explain, did they see my scars, the baby?"

Cedric squeezed her arm and kissed it, then her forehead and hushed her.

"Calm down, it's okay, it's okay, everything is fine. Hush there miss tough girl, we are okay now, safe in the city and just thirty minutes from your and Betty's new house. Don't worry, she will explain it all to you. We said she is your cousin and her sister Mercy came in as your guardian so everyone is safe, but I really wanted to call your folks. You are not okay," he added. Ruthie seemed to be in deep thought, she did not even notice Betty wake up and come to her side.

"I sleep for one minute and you've already broken her. How are you sweetie? Are you okay? Did he tell you the good news? We are housemates! Well, with the size of my house I call it roommates, instead. You're welcome, hun, all my delicious food for free," she added, smiling. At the mention of food, Ruthie felt a sudden pang of hunger. Betty saw it in her eyes and poured her a mug of porridge which was a bit warm and had no sugar. She quickly ate it and requested another, much to everyone's delight. The nurse had told them to give her the porridge in case she woke up and was talking. She then took some water and asked them to help her up. She felt a slight pain in her lower abdomen. They carefully put a pillow under her back and head and she sat down as the nurse came in smiling. She introduced herself and started checking her vitals. "Hi there, I am Mukami, your nurse. How long have you been awake? Okay, I can see the porridge is all gone. Well done, that is a good sign."

"Well I am eating for two, my baby has been starving for four days I hear." Ruthie responded in a smile as the whole room froze. Even Betty seemed dodgy.

The nurse drew the curtain around Ruthie's bed and asked for some privacy but Betty would not budge. She went beside Ruthie and held her hand.

"Ruthie, remember how that son of- well, remember how we hate your now ex-boyfriend?" Mukami shook her head in sorrow and raised her hand to stop her.

"Please, let me do this." Ruthie was crying fresh hot tears. "I am sorry but you lost your baby. The blow to your abdomen was the last straw considering how much trauma you had been through for the past months. Also, the infection was affecting the situation, but we are glad that you came back to us. You are stable and with an amazing supportive family here. Don't worry, we take good care of young ladies like you who have been through what you have. We even have a program that allows you to come and talk about your situation and we will help you through it. Ruthie, you are not alone."

She was uncontrollably crying in Betty's chest who was now rubbing her own teary eyes. Cedric had excused himself. After a few sobs and moans and hushes, the kind nurse left the two to catch up as she noticed that Ruthie had no idea what exactly went down that day. Mukami called Cedric in, who made slow hesitant steps towards the bed. His eyes were bloodshot and worry was written all over his face despite the fake smile he tried to put up. "We thought you had us for backup, turns out we need to hire you in case of anything." He giggled as he sat on the bed next to her. "Seriously boo, are you okay?" he asked as he pulled her against his side and kissed her forehead again. Betty squeezed her other arm, affection in her eyes. This was her family. She felt tears roll down her cheeks again.

"No, these are happy tears. I love you guys, and you really mean a lot to me. Thanks for not calling my parents, you would all be in jail right now." They all laughed. They all knew that Ruthie's parents would have taken extremely drastic measures which Ruthie thought would be unwarranted. She felt like they did not understand her, nor her relationship. It was complicated.

"So, what really happened after I slapped that piece of garbage?"

Betty immediately responded, jumping from the bed as if she was waiting for the opening. "Slapped? Hahaha! You did not slap nobody girl, it was martial combat! By the time we came to your side he was down and out! There were shoes, glasses, bottles, hands, and legs all over. Not even the bouncers could touch you! I am staying on your good side from now on. What did he say to you for you to explode like that? We thought you were just talking?" Cedric was laughing so hard and Ruthie was smiling weakly as she held her stomach, trying not to laugh. She still felt a bit weak and fragile.

Betty was too dramatic. She was short and a bit masculine. She had played basketball and hockey during her high school days and also tried her hand in football. In the university, she joined the ladies' basketball team. She said sports were her second love, after food. She was also a bit of a comedian; everyone called her the female Kevin Hart. She dramatized with fake karate and Kung-Fu moves as she explained. The visitors by the opposite bed drew their curtains as they smiled and shook their heads.

"I'm officially done with you. I think I need a more reliable source," she said laughing.

"Unfortunately, boo, that's kind of what happened. You broke a bottle and hit his head with it then you rained kicks, punches, and slaps all over him. He tried to defend himself by pushing you away. Unfortunately, he punched you in the stomach. You started screaming and took off your shoes, hitting him with them and in defense, he tried punching and pushing but you hit him with the pointy part in the head when he tried pinning you down. We did not know you were that strong. You then pushed him off when he hit his head and lost consciousness. You were headed towards him with your bloody heel in your hand when I carried you off, and you passed out before we even reached the room. I had to bring you to hospital, you were bleeding and we didn't know what to do. I brought you here and Betty and Mercy checked you in. The rest I think you know."

Ruthie was hearing this in shock as none of these activities registered in her mind.

"So, he didn't beat me up? What happened to him?"

"Well as much as I hate the guy, I was obligated to drop him to the nearby hospital and told them it was a bar fight and explained the situation. Betty had called Omendi, Otieno's best friend, and he was no longer our problem, but he was discharged in two days. Betty and I went to collect your things from the house. We told him you died. Well, Betty did." They had brought her to this hospital as it catered for victims of domestic violence at close to no cost. Cedric assisted where necessary and Mercy, as motherly as she was, was always there when she came from work.

Betty then asked in a serious tone, "Okay I am curious, what did he say to you that made you snap?"

Ruthie gave it a thought and laughed, "Well, he said something minor, but I think my crazy was just too much. He said he would bend me on his lap and spank me right there and I would do nothing. He called me weak." Some emotion flashed over her eyes as her forehead creased. Then it disappeared.

"Way to show him your strength, girl," Betty said as she went in for a high five. Mercy came in the room and smiled at them.

"Glad to see you with some life and joy. How are you today, Mohammed Ali?" They all laughed. Mercy went to her side and hugged her. She then sanitized her hands and took out a bucket of KFC chicken with fries for everyone. "I heard this is your favorite and you must be starving. Let's dig in."

Betty was the first to wash her hands and reach for the chicken when Mercy slapped her hand away.

"Let the invalid take the first piece, God! You have been overeating since that day and she has been starving. Glutton!" Betty made a face as Cedric stood up to clean his hands, too. They hurriedly ate, knowing well that should the medics find them they would be in deep trouble. The food was finished within no time as they were munching away as if they had not seen food for months. Mercy quickly disposed of the trash and they laughed.

"Please excuse us, we need to have some time with the patient." Said Mukami their nurse as she walked in with another medic. Ruthie's friends said their goodbyes and promised to visit the next morning.

"This is Dr. Ella, she is a therapist. We thought you would want to have a word with her, given the circumstances of your situation."

"I'm okay, I'm over it. Plus, I already have my shrink, so?" Ruthie responded as she pulled the covers over her head.

"Would you want to contact your therapist then?"

She thought for a while then sat up. "Actually no, it's okay. What do you want us to talk about?"

"Okay I'll leave you two then." Said Mukami, smiling as she left.

Dr. Ella sat on her bed and smiled at her. Then in low tones started, "I'm sorry you lost your baby; how are you holding up?"

"Well I'm kind of relieved, to be honest, I really don't want any piece of that man anywhere near me. I'm sorry to say, but I think it was God's hand."

"How was your relationship with him? Had you planned for this pregnancy?"

"Honestly Doc, I really don't want to talk about him. I just prefer letting his memory die. I have mastered the act of blocking things in my memory; don't interfere with the process."

"It's okay, we all have our coping mechanisms. Do you feel a loss or emptiness? It's a natural feeling, Ruthie. I can help you through it."

"Doc, I really wasn't living my life and never once pictured myself as a mother. All I feel is relief and freedom. Please don't push it. I don't want to talk about it and I want the memory to fade. Forever."

"Okay, okay. But here is my card, in case you ever want to talk about it. I wish you a quick recovery." The doctor responded as she handed her the card and smiled.

"I'm really sorry if I offended you, but I'm not really in a mood to talk about it. I would rather forget about it. I really appreciate your efforts."

"It's okay, now get some rest and don't hesitate to call." With that, the therapist left, and she only saw her when she was discharged, where she said goodbye. She never spoke about the loss of her baby and preferred locking the memory where she kept all her misadventures.

This was the foundation of Betty and Ruthie's close bond. The event made Betty realize that hell hath no fury like Ruthie scorned. Betty always made sure she stayed on her good side and was always there to make sure she was in check, as Ruthie did for her in return.

As she flashed back to these events and how much Betty meant to her, the speaker for the day was still telling them that they are Deborahs of the modern world and that they should rise. They were going through the book of Judges and she was too distracted. Her phone dinged, indicating a text, *"Yo, Deborah, awake from your daydream and arise, God can see through your evil fantasies and He is telling me to tell you to focus or else!* It was from Betty. She smiled and responded, *"Tell Him I will tell you all about it after the session, (winky face emoji)"*

The session was really long and informative and as usual Ruthie tried the best she could to focus on the sermon and make sense of it so she could apply it in her normal life. She even ignored what she deemed to be inapplicable or "toxic religiousness." After the final prayer, Betty was by her side. People were mingling as announcements were made. Some of their former schoolmates were there, surprised that these two would come for actual Christian meetings and go for missions on their own volition. She then got a text and responded, smiling. Betty snatched her phone from her, "Ethan? 'Hope you arrived on time. I have more nuts to share in case you want some?' Speak girl! What nuts? Where are you coming from and why haven't I heard of these nuts before?" Ruthie snatched her phone back, hushing her. "Ruthie! I demand answers right now! Are you coming to the Holy presence of God fresh from fornication?" Ruthie had to hit her in the arm for her to shut up.

"It's not what you think. He's my new friend. We met yesterday in the *matatu* here and my aunt was not available at the time. It was late, okay? He offered me a place in his house where we slept regular sleep. He is really nice and hospitable and weird, imposing, and so annoying." Betty could not believe her friend; she met someone in a public vehicle and slept in his house on the same day? Within hours?

"Have you learnt nothing from movies and our own lives? Are you going crazy again?" she scolded.

"Well, I am going nuts," she said, winking at her friend as they laughed.

Then she told her friend all about him and she invited herself to the upcoming ice cream date. "I am not going to let you get sucked into another psycho's life. I have to vet this Ethan guy." Ruthie knew that she did this for her own good and also, she believed that if anyone could see beyond a man's bullshit, it had to be Betty. They gossiped all through their lunch break as they ate and when the afternoon prayer session came, they decided to sit far apart so as to not distract each other. After that, they both went to Ruthie's aunt's and spent the night catching up, then left the next day each to her own home. Ethan was consistently checking up on Ruthie and conversation flowed naturally. She actually enjoyed talking to him.

CHAPTER THREE

Perfectly Imperfect

RUTHIE WAS BACK AT HOME in her room strategizing and organizing. Her internship was coming to an end in two weeks and she had a feeling that she should plan her life, set some goals, and just have a fresh start. She felt like her life was all over the place and confused. She had read several self-help books from her sessions at the hospital, and from the support group she had been part of for the past year or so. Betty would accompany her to some of these sessions as most of them were interactive and she actually learned a lot of life skills there. She would often tell Ruthie that she felt like she was actually learning more than her. Ruthie, on the other hand, found herself ranting about anything and everything during these sessions at first and then on several occasions when she would fall back to her "below rock bottom" cocoon. Whenever it was her turn to share or even introduce herself, she found herself spiraling and talking nonstop about her miserable life and who hurt her, or she would be frustrated trying to explain who she was and why she was the way she was, or she would tell her friends how life was and asked them whether that was the way to go in life. She always felt trapped and confused in all aspects of her life. She would gain too much weight due to stress-eating and everyone brought it up so much that everyone suddenly became an expert in her life, telling her what to do and what not to do. She hated life and everyone. She hated herself.

She threw all her clothes to the ground and started folding and sorting one by one. She then arranged her dressing table, cleaned out her suitcases, removed the cobwebs from her ceiling and scrubbed every inch of her room clean. She then went and washed her laundry, then took a long hot shower and made herself her favorite dish of the season- well, the easiest to make- shepherd's pie. She felt good about herself when she made the dishes she loved and ate them in the freedom of her solitude. She felt comfortable and free whenever she was in this state. Nobody was there to tell her to finish her food, there was no pressure about what and how much she ate, and above all, the wheels in her brain productively turned and churned. It was an amazing feeling. She took out her diary and started writing down her goals and plans as she sipped her rosemary tea. She felt energized. As she wrote it all down, she remembered that God was the only reason she was not in a mental asylum, or so she was made to believe.

This was the only hope and belief she could hold onto that distracted her from her actual life. She believed that her faith was solely based on the fact that she desperately needed to hang on to something, anything, to keep her sane. Religion had various beliefs and practices that would actually work in the normal day to day life, like prayer, kindness, humility (within reason), fellowship for distraction, and also to make one feel like their life was not that bad compared to others. Encouragement, self-love and worth; she used really whatever it was it seemed to work in her life at that moment. She felt rejuvenated each time she would turn to her religion.

She was done laying down her life goals, plans, and ideas. She then started writing self-affirmations. These are the words she would repeat to herself to make her feel better and a bit powerful. Right now, she felt like she could take on the entire world, and writing them now when feeling that powerful was a plus. She then started crafting. She took two tiny boxes and decorated them with glitter pens and colored papers. On one she wrote "Answered Prayers" and on another she wrote "Prayer Requests." She then wrote prayer requests, folded them neatly and put them in the second box. She then decided to open them exactly one year later. She felt content and happy. Existing in this kind of life was distraction enough to take her through the remaining year in the university and push her to her fully adult life. And if by chance God actually paid attention to those things, He would give her a job and a future she wanted. She would rather live in that bubble than expose herself to the uncertainty of real life.

She realized no one had called or texted her the whole time and wondered where her phone was. Her two brothers were returning home today and she had not heard from any of them, not even her sisters or overbearing mother. In all honesty, she was really looking for her phone because of Ethan. They had not seen each other since the groundnut day but constantly talked and chatted. They now knew a lot about each other and each time she felt like he was becoming a bit too flirtatious, she would push the brakes. She had her guard so high up and so solid, not even she could break it. Ethan was often worried about her defenses and he sensed a story there, but he did not know how to bring it up. Ruthie, on the other hand, was so scared about the feelings she had for Ethan that she kept reinforcing her guard. He made her smile, laugh, and feel so angry. He was real and not perfect. Ethan was not afraid of his flaws and embraced them; he even shared them with her. He never once hid who he was in Ruthie's point of view. Ruthie admired this about him. She often tried to get his view on what an ideal life should be like, but he would brush it off stating that there really was no one way of living life. Everyone is unique and has their own path. It often puzzled her. Ethan often told her that it was dangerous to mold life in accordance to one particular life coach or society; she risked losing her identity that way. He often told her that she was a masterpiece and unique and amazing just the way she was. Her flaws defined her and made her beautiful. Ruthie pretended to agree with him but deep down she knew that she would not risk it. She knew how ugly her real life was and how grotesque her flaws could be, and she did not even want to think about her hideous scars.

Ethan's view on Christianity was also attractive to Ruthie. He believed that it was a personal journey and he could do whatever he felt was right. He trusted his gut and believed his conscience. He partied, had fun, and interacted with people but also had the purest of hearts. He was kind to strangers and loved children, he believed in kindness and karma. He also told Ruthie never to be hard on herself for anything, that God never made a perfect person so the best was to do your best and live life to the fullest. He occasionally prayed. Ethan never beat himself up as much as Ruthie thought a person should. The concept was too risky for Ruthie. What if she lived her best life and ended up screwing up? She often disagreed with Ethan and when he felt her anger rising, he would not back down and play safe like other people in her life did. He would let her unleash her full wrath and feelings about their argument and then when she was done, he would ask her how that felt, just venting her pent-up feelings and stating her opinions without a care and standing by them no matter what. She would feel patronized. Then after she cooled down, they would talk and laugh. However, there were days when they would avoid certain topics just for the peace of it, especially when they had been fighting too much.

Ethan had been fascinated by Ruthie. At first it had been because of the striking resemblance she had to the first love of his life, Hadassah. She was a nurse, strong willed, and opinionated. She had her life planned out. They were so in love and even moved in together back during their time at university. Ethan was not keen on Christianity or going to church and she really insisted that he joined her every Saturday to go to church with her. At first, he refused to go and gave excuses, but soon the excuses ran out and he found it easier to just join her at church. She then insisted that he stopped drinking and bringing alcohol to the house. He stopped drinking and going out but would occasionally hide a bottle of beer in his closet and enjoy it when she was not in the house. It got worse when she incorporated cookouts with her couple friends, retreats with the Adventist friends, and even hinted that in two months they would start couple counselling at their church. Ethan felt lonely and invisible in his own life. He was only twenty-five and lived like a forty-year-old with kids. He felt like he was missing out on life. Yes, his life was together and healthy and even "right with God," or whatever that meant, but he was not happy. He loved Hadassah with all of his heart and liked how she lived her life but he hated their life together. He was depressed and needed his friends, parties, and above all, his life. All the ideas he suggested were quickly shot down by Hadassah the Perfectionist and he really got annoyed but did not want to argue with her.

One time, his mother fell ill and he had to travel but was short on fare. Hadassah was happy to pitch in and he left immediately. He stayed home for more than a week and felt great about it. He felt free and loved and he felt like he mattered. Hadassah called daily and even talked to his mother on several occasions. When it was time to go back, Ethan did not feel like it and kept postponing it with the excuse of helping his mother. His mother then noticed what was going on and decided to ask him.

His mother retrieved five liters of boxed wine and Ethan hesitated a bit until his mother told him to loosen up and talk to her. They drank the wine slowly as her mother eased the topic in. Then she asked how Hadassah was. Ethan had already had three glasses of wine and was feeling great. When his mother asked him how he really felt, all his feelings tumbled out and he expressed how suffocated he felt and how he hated his life, himself, and even school. He talked for close to an hour straight without interruption.

His mother smiled at him when he stopped and caught his breath. He was crying and didn't even know it. His mother stood up and embraced him. He had not felt this good in a long time. He felt a weight lifted from his chest and shoulders. His mind felt so clear. There and then he knew that he had lost himself in the name of love and he needed to find himself again. "You know what to do, don't you? Talk to her," his mother advised, and he just nodded.

The next day, he went back to the city and they had the talk. He explained how he felt about the relationship, how he needed his own friends and bubble, he needed to live his life without her planning it out, including the dress code. He also felt suffocated and hated the Seventh Day Adventist Church and what they believed in. Hadassah could not believe her ears.

"If you have been feeling this way all this time, why did you not say it? You hate visiting my mom every other weekend?" she asked angrily. "But I told you it's tradition! My brothers do it with their girlfriends. It is the best way to guide us through this courtship period."

"Courtship? We have been dating for, what, less than a year? Do you even know who I am and what I stand for?"

It was then that they both realized that it was best they parted ways.

Ethan had learned from that experience to always live his truth and express himself his way. He also decided to live life to the fullest on his own terms. If he could coexist with different types of friends with different characters and lifestyles, then should he get a girl in his life, they should be able to embrace their differences, complement their life choices, and above all, enjoy their similarities. He vowed never again to lose himself and never to allow himself to impose his life choices on anyone either. For this reason, he felt like Ruthie was fragile and needed someone to help her through life. He felt like she was imprisoned and afraid. He knew someone broke her, so her guard was always up. He felt the need to show her his flaws and imperfect life just so she could show him hers, but she never budged.

He knew that the whole Christianity-angle she took in certain aspects of her life was a front for something, but what? At this point, he was no longer interested in having her as a girlfriend, but rather as a friend. She needed a friend. She had this best friend Betty who in Ethan's opinion, was not the best friend; she was as scared as Ruthie was, or maybe was the same person as her, which did them more harm than good. "Two blind girls crossing the highway," as he always put it in his mind.

As they chatted away, Ruthie felt different, energized and happy. She felt motivated and excited. It was not only about her brothers coming home; she loved her family, but also enjoyed her own space which was limited whenever they were all at home. Normally she would complain and sulk all day when they came but today was different. Ethan was happy when she was. Ethan started his flirtatious talk just to gauge the situation, Ruthie went along with it. After a while he called her to make sure he had the right girl. They talked and talked for close to an hour until she heard a car horn. "That's my family here to burst my bubble. I wish I was there with you," Ruthie said over the phone.

Ethan felt his pants get tighter. "Don't worry, it will be okay. I am just a call away. Don't keep them waiting, I will be online." As he hung up, his heart was warm and his mind was running wild. He quickly ran to take a cold shower and then wrote in his diary, "*I have found the mother of my children, she's my missing rib.*" His mother called, asking him to go visit. It had been close to a month since he last went home and he did not notice it. He always felt at home just talking to Ruthie over the phone, chatting with her and watching movies with her virtually, listening to the music she recommended. He always looked forward to going home at the end of the day or spending weekends at home just so he could talk to Ruthie on phone. He was as lost in her world as she was in his and they were both scared about it.

Ethan decided to go home the next weekend and found his mother had gone over the top to prepare his favorite dishes and stocked up on food and drinks. He was the only son to his single mother and he absolutely adored her. He remembered one time when Hadassah's brother hinted that the whole reason they met at their home was to show him what an ideal and complete family actually was. He had felt so offended about it and when he tried to tell Hadassah about it, she defended her brother, stating that it was important for him to see what fathers do in homesteads and what she needed in a family. He wondered why he never saw the signs during all those times. His mother had always warned him about Hadassah and her family but was always afraid that if she argued with him about it too much that he would feel the need to prove his mother wrong. Thus, she waited for him to realize himself, of course with a little of her guidance. She believed she raised a strong man, principled and loving.

The only downside to Ethan was that he believed in people and had an extremely big heart, and it cost him. His mother was actually glad she let him make the mistakes he did, especially with Hadassah. She hated that self-righteous girl, especially when she had the audacity to question her faith and her parenting abilities.

"Why do you choose to be a single mother and raise a boy? Don't you think he needs a father figure, a man to guide him through the issues of life?" asked Hadassah one day when they had gone to visit Ethan's mother.

"Young girl, that is none of your business. You have absolutely no right to meddle into my affairs. Doesn't your bible say anything about respecting your elders?" his mother responded, annoyance written all over her face as she stood and left for the kitchen. "I think it's time for you to leave, it's getting late." She released them that day and really hoped that Ethan would see the kind of girl he was dating and break it off. She hated her guts and could not wait for the day when he finally learnt his lesson and rid himself of her. She was not one to make decisions for his son like all mothers-in-law but she wanted what was best for him. He had made mistakes before, but Hadassah was the greatest. She was the only one that made his mother pray for Ethan. Each time she felt like meddling in the relationship, she would take out her rosary and pray.

The only other time she prayed this much was when she was expectant with Ethan's little sister, Molly. She was ten years Ethan's junior. Her father, just like Ethan's, took off just after birth and she had never talked about it again. Molly was a breach baby. They had no finances for a caesarian section and she felt like both their lives were at risk. She even went to a traditional midwife to help her turn the baby at thirty-six weeks; the midwife had said that the baby would turn if she went to her to help her with the birthing process. It was a difficult situation for her. Luckily, when she went into labor at thirty-eight weeks, her great aunt was present and acted as her doula. She labored for thirteen hours until her water broke and she had to have an emergency operation. Her great aunt was gracious enough to top up her bill with little help from the nurse attendant who talked to the hospital accountant to waive a percentage of the hospital bill, and to her that was the greatest miracle.

This experience taught Ms. Amari, Ethan's mother, of saving culture. She opened two accounts for both her children when Molly turned one and deposited money every week from whatever she had gotten from her many hustles. She had a fixed amount that she would faithfully deposit. Even when times were tough, she would rather walk from town to their house, deny herself new outfits, and even ate an unbalanced diet or one meal per day, but never did she ever fail to deposit the amount. She never withdrew that money either and told herself that she could not rob her own children of their future. Ethan would often tell her that he would help educate Molly just so his mother could rest, but she told him to father his own children and educate them on his own terms.

Ethan adored his baby sister. He took one and a half years off of school just to support his family and assist with the bills despite his mother's protests. He pretended to be conflicted about his course choices until his mother gave him an ultimatum: go to school or move out. He kept telling his mother that the fund was not going anywhere and should he want to enroll to university, he would. This was the time to give back to his family as the junior man of the house. He referred to his mother as the main man.

His mother noticed a difference in Ethan's behavior. He was always on his phone and she occasionally caught him daydreaming about something. He was often distracted and kept asking his mother about female psychology and such questions. He was seated in the kitchen supposedly helping his mother make dinner when his mother asked him how his internship was going on.

"Did they say they will retain you as a part-time worker? I really want you to be busy this coming academic year as you are only remaining with your project and is it four units? This is the time to set a good foundation for your career. Pass me the salt," she stated as she stirred the pot of mixed vegetables.

"By the way mom, if, say, a girl tells you that she has migraines besides the normal cramps during her time of the month and she faints and has bouts of memory loss; is that from trauma or is she okay? Should she see a doctor for that?" Ethan asked, neither looking up from his phone nor budging from the counter he was leaning against as he chatted away. His mother snatched his phone from him in annoyance.

"Ethan! Would you give it a break? What's the point of coming home if you are going to be an online doctor and ignore the rest of the world? My rules are clear, no phones in my kitchen," she said as she put the phone in her apron pocket and went ahead to grab the salt herself.

"I'm sorry mum, don't be mad," he said as he went to rinse his hands in the sink. "It's just, I met this girl some time back and mom, she really has captured me. She is so broken, and-" his mother turned sharply at him.

"Eiy! What are you saying right now? You want to now go around repairing broken girls in the city? Did you learn nothing from Hadassah? Ethan, there is nobody who can repair a broken person. Who repaired me? Who is going to repair you once *you* become broken again? Have you even healed from the past heartbreak? Ah-ah, you are not ready. Please. No!" she shouted at him. Molly, who was on midterm, came rushing into the kitchen.

"What is it now? Ethan, you've not even been here for twenty-four hours already-" she started.

"Shut up, none of you were here for the past I don't know how long and you are already getting on my nerves. You are overcrowding my kitchen. Please go. Ah-ah! Leave!" she interrupted, throwing her hands around, not even bothering to look at them. They scurried out of the kitchen like rats. They knew better than to contest their mother when she was in that mood.

"You had to annoy her on the first day back, now she won't even take us to Village Inn for a fun day tomorrow. You are such a-" Molly blamed.

"Such a what?" Ethan asked, chasing Molly around the sitting room. "Come back here, you stupid girl, I want to hear what kind of a 'such a' I am. Come here!" They pushed the dining chairs so roughly that one fell down.

"Eeeh! Break everything and leave, that's what you know best." Their mom shouted from the kitchen sarcastically.

They stopped and sat down in the living area as Ethan grabbed the remote control and changed the channel. "Comedy Central? That's new. Who is she?" Molly teased.

"Eh shut up, that is what got us into this mess to begin with," he responded, then made a lock and key gesture on his lips.

After dinner, their mother had calmed down and they were catching up talking about everything and anything, carefully evading the topic of Ethan's new 'girlfriend'. Molly and Ethan cleaned the kitchen and the dishes as their mother retired to bed.

The next day, Ethan woke up to a song that he had heard from Ruthie a while ago which he had not paid attention to then. It was *When God Made You,* by Natalie Grant. "When God made you, He must have been thinking of me." He was streaming the song on repeat until he decided to download it and set it as Ruthie's special ringtone. He was smiling the whole time, and each time a new stanza came on, no matter how many times he listened to it, he could feel a fresh set of powerful butterflies fluttering in his stomach. He called Ruthie and she had the most soothing morning phone voice ever. It always made Ethan look forward to an amazing day ahead. He knew that it was going to be a fantastic day. Ruthie even prayed with him over the phone for a great day and he did not mind it. She was thoughtful and unimposing; she always requested his permission first and told him it would be a great experience for them both. She even prayed for Ethan's family and looked forward to someday meeting the "cheeky Molly" as Ethan described her. They had grown so fond of each other that they even affected each other's mood. Not a day had gone by without them talking to each other- not even the gloomy days.

Ethan was so afraid that Ruthie would never let her guard down and thus never experience the true and pure love he felt for her. She was conflicted and disturbed and so scared of something. He could tell that she was also afraid of not being a perfect human being. She dreaded missing out on certain aspects of life and ended up missing the beauty of the wholesome flow of her own. He felt like fixing her, like holding her forever and letting her know that she was safe and complete by herself, that she could live her own full life and he would keep her safe. If only he could talk to someone about it, especially his mother.

The next day, their mother woke up in a good mood and they were laughing away as they ate breakfast prepared by Molly to butter their mum up for the family outing. They dressed up and went for lunch at The Shepherd's Hotel and Grill. After they had ordered their roasted goat meat, Ethan ordered a beer for himself and some wine for his mother. Molly had to order a soda due to her age but her mother allowed her an occasional glass of wine, which she preferred to drink after the meal. "So, tell me about her then," his mother prompted as she took a sip from her second glass, not really looking Ethan in the eye. Ethan felt his heart skip a beat.

"Okay, her name is Ruthie, we met around three months ago in a *matatu*." His mother shot him an unsure glance. "I know what you want to say but just hear me out. She studies communications and public relations and she is an amazing woman, mom. She is sweet, innocent and lovely- well, she's a bit fragile but she's perfect, mom. She slept in my house the first day since we arrived late in the city because her aunt was asleep by the time we arrived there. She is Christian, but very open discussing one's personal relationship with God, she does not impose and is just, I can't explain, all around wonderful." He finished smiling fondly as he toyed with his glass. His mother knew there and then that he was in love and so did Molly. Right on cue, Ruthie called; it was a video call and the whole table was smiling when he answered.

"Hi there, how are you feeling today?" Ethan asked.

"I'm okay, where are you? That doesn't look like your house, my dear. How I wish I could escape from here, my brothers are overbearing," she responded.

"I'm actually at The Shepherd's Hotel and Grill with my family, do you want to say hi?" he asked.

"Oh my God, no! I'm sorry, you could have told me, are they there now? I'm not prepared," she responded, attempting to straighten her hair and rub her eyes.

"Hi Ruthie!" his mother and Molly shouted in the background, as Ethan laughed while turning the camera to face them.

"Hi, I'm so sorry to intrude, I didn't-" she responded as she felt heat rising in her cheeks.

His mother grabbed the phone. "Oh no, no, no please, come join us, I hear you live in town. That's what, thirty minutes away? Plus, we heard you could use some time out." She winked at her as Molly came to the camera's view.

"Oh no, I am not ready right now," she responded.

"I don't really want to take no for an answer. Get ready and Ethan will send you something for a taxi. We have ordered enough food for two more people, please join us. I promise you will be back home by dark," his mother persuaded.

"Okay ma'am, let me get ready and inform my parents. I will be there in like an hour or so; I'm really sorry to intrude." She blushed harder.

His mother hung up, much to Ethan's shock. She smiled and slid the phone towards Ethan. "Easy peasy."

Molly was over the moon. Ethan could feel his heartbeat in his ears. He could not believe his mother's guts- he really wanted to take it slow with Ruthie because of the issues she had. He knew his mother meant well but really, why would she do that? Was it the wine, or was she just curious? He could not ask his mother to stop meddling in his life; he knew better than to spoil her mood again- the milk was already spilt anyway.

Ethan's mother looked at Ethan and instantly knew that he was tensed up and angry, perhaps a little disappointed in her. Part of her felt bad about it, but she consoled herself with the fact that she needed to protect him. But from what? Love? Heartbreaks or more disappointments? He was a grown man and he should handle his own business, but he needed his mother. She wanted to apologize but could not bring herself to show weakness, so she just continued drinking her wine. "Have you sent her the money yet?" asked Molly, trying to break the tense silence. Ethan took his phone and sent Ruthie the money then called the waiter for another beer.

"Ethan, you know I'm just looking out for you, right? Plus, she sounds so lovely, I really wanted to meet her. I promise we will behave ourselves and not force anything. Right, Molly?" his mother prompted as she tried to hold his hand. He pulled away, not even looking up. "Come on, look at us at least. Give us some ground rules then."

At that, Ethan looked up and said, "You know, we are still just friends, she is scared of relationships or even getting close. I really worked hard to be where we are right now and what you guys did was really not cool. Now she will start thinking that this was my plan all along, to trick her into meeting my family and smother her with all this baggage then-" he paused and looked down, a vein popping on his temple.

"Look, we can call the twins here and Molly's classmate, what's her name? So that we can be a whole party and she won't feel 'smothered' by your over-caring family," his mother piped in as she took out her phone and started calling her best friend and neighbor, Mrs. Vaughn. She was a German lady initially married to their Kenyan neighbor. Her husband was rarely around and only visited once or twice a year. He worked in the legal field and was always travelling for work. Mrs. Vaughn and Ms. Amari had raised their children together, borrowing notes from each other and sharing. She had given birth to twins around the same time that Ethan was born, and it took a toll on her. She had tubal litigation after she gave birth. Her husband left after that, claiming he had another family and would like to have more children, which ended up breaking their little haven. That was when they became even closer with Ethan's mother due, and they often provided support for each other. They were happy to join in, and even offered to pick up Molly's friend on the way.

Ethan was restless; he kept checking his phone and the entrance of the Inn. He then remembered Ruthie's reservations about alcohol and ordered water for her. His mother had never seen him this nervous before, which made her even more curious about this girl.

Suddenly his phone rang and it was her saying that she had arrived. He went and met her at the gate. He could not believe his eyes. He felt his heart skip several beats as his breath was caught in his throat. She was dressed in a simple yellow sundress with strappy silver sandals and had a pink sweater that matched with her flowery sling bag. She had minimal makeup on that brought out her facial features and a slim silver necklace with a small butterfly pendant that hung just right, complimenting her exquisite long neck. She smiled shyly at Ethan who was still in a daze.

"Are you going to say hi or are you just going to stand there staring?" she asked, moving to hug him.

Ethan then pulled out of his trance and smiled at her. "I'm sorry, you look amazingly beautiful today. I'm so sorry about my family, I promise it was not my plan to ambush you like that. I am as equally surprised as you are," he said after hugging her, still holding her hand.

"Look who is in love, is this why we are here? You two look awesome together, I could just eat you up!" he heard a familiar voice right behind Ruthie and before he could answer, Ms. Vaughn had already scooped tiny Ruthie in a tight bear hug. One of the twins, Jack, put an arm around his shoulders as he watched the ladies while Derrick punched him on the side of his arm.

"Nice work man. She is so beautiful that my eyes hurt," he said, winking at Ethan.

Molly's friend Debbie zoomed past them as she went to find the rest of the party. Ruthie was really confused and shot Ethan an accusing glance as he mouthed the words "I'm sorry" to her. The boys were already leading him towards their table while Ms. Vaughn hogged Ruthie all to herself.

When they arrived at the table, everyone was shouting and hugging and greeting as Ethan just stared longingly at Ruthie. All this seemed like a dream to him. She blended so well with everyone as she introduced herself to his family and laughed along with them, taking in compliments and giving out her own. Ethan was worried about the alcohol, knowing of her reservations but she seemed not to mind. She looked comfortable, blended even. She was given the seat next to Ethan and he took a deep breathe inhaling her perfume as if his life depended on it, hoping he was discreet.

"Don't be creepy, you freak! I saw that." Molly pointed at him and he threw a bottle top at her, telling her to be quiet. When everyone had settled down, the waiter came and took their drink orders as she confirmed with them about their food quantity. Everyone gave their orders and much to everyone's surprise, Ethan asked for more water. "You know I don't mind it if you want a beer or something, feel free to be you. I think I will have some wine after food. You know, to ease all this tension," Ruthie mumbled near his ear.

"No, it's okay, I already had some beer earlier. Plus, I would like to be sober when I witness you drinking that wine," he replied in a whisper as he smiled after the last statement. They drank and ate while they chatted away, not even noticing how the time flew.

Ruthie even found herself ordering a third glass of wine as she let loose.

Ruthie bonded so well with Ethan's mother and her and Molly joked around like real siblings; they even bickered at some point. She did not remember being this free and happy in a long time. She felt so relaxed and Ethan could see it in the glow. Ruthie totally adored how Ethan's eyes lit up whenever they conversed with his mother and how he cared for his sister. She envied their family dynamic and was falling in love with the entire family.

"Ruthie, now that you have met our entire clan, tell us about your family," Ethan's mother prompted.

"Okay, I am the third born in a family of seven, two elder brothers who are both working in the medical field, and the youngest are twin girls, currently in university. One is studying law while the other one is into International relations, much like my parents."

Ms. Vaughn and Ethan's mother exchanged a look that Ethan noticed.

"So, middle child, huh? Is it true that you are the most misunderstood and the black sheep in your family?" Molly asked.

Ethan reprimanded her while Ruthie laughed, brushing it off. "Yes, well, more or less. That is the universal definition of a middle child, just like last-borns are the most spoilt and annoying of all siblings," she shot back, gaining howls and snaps from the boys. She had missed this. They laughed at the disses.

"So, your parents are lawyers?" Ethan's mother continued, while Ethan creased his brow at her. "No, my father is a retired judge, while my mother is a human rights activist. She worked with the United Nations and right now she freelances. You may have heard of her, Pamela Chuma? She mostly deals with children's rights and other pro bono outreach programs in the county, mostly just legal aid services."

The table went silent. Everyone was showing discomfort and Ruthie wondered whether she had said the wrong thing and looked at Ethan for help. Ethan had beads of sweat on his forehead. How had he missed all this? Had he never asked about her parents before? Did he already know and had just ignored the facts or was he just plain stupid? He was at a loss. In fact, everybody was. Molly excused herself and asked Debbie to go check something out at the back. The twins both had matching sets of veins on their foreheads while the mothers took gulps of wine from their glasses. Ethan's leg was shaking.

"Did I say something wrong? Is everything okay?" she asked, not able to hold it in any longer. One could cut through the tension with a knife.

"I'm sorry Ruthie, it's not you honey. So, your dad must be James Chuma, right? How is he doing?" Ms. Vaughn asked while the twins both stood up to go to the washroom. Ruthie knew there and then that this was politics. "He is well, just enjoying his retirement. I'm sorry if I revealed something sensitive, I did not mean to do it. I'm really sorry, Ms. Amari," she said apologetically towards Ethan's mother who was now silent. "Did he decide against one of your cases? Is it my mother? Please forgive us for whatever it was. I'm sure it was purely business-" She did not know why she was apologizing for whatever it was that dampened the mood of the party. Her parents had made a lot of enemies in the course of their careers as they were fierce and no nonsense when it came to work. They were the reason Ruthie hated anything to do with the law or the so-called "justice system-" someone always ended up hurt. "Look, whatever it was, I also don't support a lot of what they do in the name of justice. Please excuse them." She was now sweating.

"Look Ruthie, don't worry about it and stop apologizing. It's not your fault," Ethan started, avoiding everyone's gaze. Ruthie could have sworn she saw balancing tears from the side of Ethan's eyes. The boys made it back to the table just as Ethan had stopped talking and they seemed to have composed themselves.

"Well, will you look at the time, I think its best that we leave now. Ethan, go find your sister so that we can finish up. We would not want to keep Ruthie for long. It was really nice to meet you, dear. You are so lovely and we would, um, like to see you again, I think," Ethan's mother said, wearing the fakest smile Ruthie had ever seen. "Please forgive us if we made you a little bit uncomfortable there. As you can see, we are a weird bunch and are quite unpredictable," she finished as Molly and Debbie walked in cautiously.

Everyone finished their drinks in awkward silence as Ms. Amari paid the bill. Ruthie called a cab and was given some money by Ethan's mother, despite her protests, which was way more than what she needed.

CHAPTER FOUR

Secrets and Lies

RUTHIE ARRIVED HOME AT AROUND seven thirty in the evening and she felt so lost. She felt like everything she had done in the past few months was in vain. She could tell what had happened that evening. What could her parents have possibly done to make the entire party feel that way, including Ethan? She had never seen him so defeated before. He looked so lost and felt like he was too close to tears. What had her family done to them? Why was she suffering, paying for the mistakes of her self-righteous parents? She went online and looked up Nelly Amari Kenya law reports, nothing came up. She then looked up Nelly Amari versus Pamela Chuma, still nothing. She even looked up Ethan's name and Molly, nothing came up. She then decided to call up Ethan to inform him that she had arrived safely. He sounded so aloof and distracted that she decided not to talk to him any further. She took a shower and went downstairs where everyone was seated, minding their business. Her mother was in the kitchen with the cook preparing dinner. She contemplated going straight to her and asking the question herself but she preferred dealing with her father first, since the freak-out only started after she mentioned who her mother was.

"Dad, hi," she started. Her father was watching some international news. He looked up, acknowledging her, then she went and sat next to him.

"What's up Ruthie, I didn't see you come in. How was your small outing with your friends?" he asked.

"It was alright," she responded, still wondering how to bring the whole thing up. "Mom has made a lot of enemies in her line of work, right? But I have not seen many female enemies, I mean, is there an instance where she could have made female enemies, like women who hate her?" she asked.

"What did you hear, kiddo? Our line of work attracts a lot of enemies and we warned you about listening to every word on the street. We are a family that protects each other. Do you see that fence? That is where-" his father started and Ruthie cut him short.

"Where we leave the outside world, and focus on what's inside. Family. I know dad, it's just that something happened today and it has me thinking a lot."

"Ruthie, why do you want to stress yourself with haters out there?" her second born brother Jabari started. "We have had a lot of enemies in the past because of dad's job. Remember what happened to you in seventh grade when you first went to boarding school? Whatever happened today I'm sure is much less than that, so lay off dad and let him enjoy his retirement." Jabari was her older brother, who was sporty and full of energy and in Ruthie's opinion, really enjoyed prying into other people's affairs. Jabari was tall and really tried hitting the gym often, so he was lean and athletic. He was never shy about his feelings and had had a fleet of girlfriends, until he settled for Chela, who he had recently proposed to.

"It's not about dad. I think this has more to do with mom than dad. And thank you so much, oh fountain of compassion. I did not need to sleep tonight, I really needed to relive my worst nightmare!" she shot back in anger. She could not believe his guts. She already had a lot on her plate and Jabari was making her remember one of the darkest times in her life. That ordeal flashed in her brain as she tried to bury them and think of the good times as advised by her psychiatrist.

"Stop it at once, Jabari! I will not condone this behavior in my house. Ruthie, whatever it is, please calm down and ignore it. You don't have to carry our burdens for us. We have developed a thick skin and you will too in good time," her father said as he rubbed her back. Her eyes were shiny with tears threatening to fall at any time.

"It is already affecting me, dad. I met this guy. He is just a friend of mine, a really good friend, and we have been talking for a while. He is pure-hearted and really amazing, dad, someone I was willing to introduce you to. Today I went and had lunch with him, his family, and his friends and when they asked about my family, the whole vibe changed after the mention of mom. We were having a great time and even bonded and all. I really don't understand what happened." She poured out her heart, crying on her father's chest.

Her father just rubbed her back and hushed her.

"What's up with her? Another heartbreak?" her eldest brother Mark asked Jabari.

"Apparently, and this time she's blaming it on mom," Jabari replied.

Ruthie was sobbing uncontrollably in her father's chest. "Whose head are we going for? Give us an address, mama," Mark said as he headed towards her. Mark was the first born. He was calm and collected and enjoyed his solitude. Mark was tall, kept his full beard but his head bald. He was also well-built, quite effortlessly as he never hit the gym, and was only sporty when having a friendly match with Jabari. He enjoyed reading books and was a tech-nerd. He had a fiancé who he kept under wraps and only brought her a few times to meet his family. Nobody dared asked him about the marriage plans- "when it's time, you'll know," he always said.

"Both of you go back to your rooms right now! I will handle this myself. In fact, don't come down until after she has slept. Nkt!" her father barked at them and they went off mumbling something about soft hearts and bad boys dying. The commotion heated up and her mother found a tense atmosphere when she came in. Her father signaled for her to wait for a bit and she nodded somberly in understanding, then left to finish making dinner.

When dinner was ready, Ruthie rose from her seat and left for her bedroom, refusing to eat. She locked herself in her room and cried herself to sleep. The situation had affected her so much that she felt like it actually physically hurt; she had switched off her phone as she felt like she needed some time alone. All night, she would cry bitterly and painfully until she dozed off, then when she woke up she would repeat the cycle. She did not leave her room even for a glass of water. When dinner time came on the next day, she could barely open her eyes, so she opted to just drift off to sleep.

She woke up on the third day after the ordeal with swollen red eyes and a dry throat. She looked at herself in the mirror and fresh tears fell. She could not believe how much this had affected her. What was it with Ethan and his family that affected her this much? She went to the shower and did not seem to stop crying. Then she dressed in warm sweats and a t-shirt then went back to bed, crying fresh tears.

Her pillow was soaked and her tear ducts seemed to keep on going. She heard a knock on her door.

"Ruthie, baby? I have some lemonade for you, can I come in?" she heard her mother ask.

"I'm not thirsty," she responded, hoarsely and barely audible.

"You have been sleeping since yesterday. When I tried to wake you up, you groaned and turned away. Please talk to me. I may be of help." Her mother opened the door slightly "Come on baby, I'm sorry to come in but we are worried about you. Oh my goodness! Are you okay?" she rushed over to her bed and held her tightly.

Her mother rocked her back and forth like a baby as she smoothed her hair with her hands. "Sshhh baby, it's going to be fine. Please don't cry. It's not your fault baby, hush."

Then she fainted.

Her mother was so scared. Ruthie had become so weak and her mouth was dry and peeling off. She tried shaking her daughter to wake her up, but she did not move. She felt Ruthie's pulse and it was too weak. She panicked.

"Honey! Mark! Jabari! Is there anyone here? Uuuwiiiiii!" she screamed. "Uuuuwwii help! Someone call the doctor!" Mark and Jabari ran to Ruthie's room.

"What's up mom, is everything okay?" Mark asked. Jabari was already on his phone, dialing their family doctor's number.

"She was crying and she passed out! Feel her pulse! My poor baby," responded her mother, hugging her tightly as she cried, Mark went over and felt her pulse.

"She is weak because she hasn't been eating. It will be fine mom."

Their father had arrived at the scene and was looking at them with worry written all over his face.

"What has the doctor said, have you described the condition in detail?" he asked Jabari.

"Yes dad, she is on her way. She said we just need to watch her and she will be here in thirty minutes tops," Jabari responded.

"I will find whoever is responsible for this and they will pay!" said Mr. Chuma, worry replaced with anger.

"Please, now is not the time for revenge; can't you see our daughter's condition?" Pamela asked, her eyes still wet with tears as two veins visibly throbbed on her temples. Her face was now entirely red. Mr. Chuma walked out of the room. The doctor arrived after forty-five minutes and she was rushed to Ruthie's room by Chuma.

"Don't worry *wakili*, she will be fine. She probably passed out because her blood sugar is too low. I understand she has not been eating?" said the doctor as she pricked Ruthie's finger to take her blood sample and put in in the gadget which beeped. "Yes, her blood sugar is low, but not so much. Has she been under stress?" she asked.

"Yes. She has been depressed but would not tell us why," replied her mother.

"Very well, this is just glucose. She also seems dehydrated, judging from her lips, so the water and electrolytes will help her. I'm going to start a line for her."

The doctor explained as she took out the injections and branular, plus a bag with some transparent liquid in it. She went on with her work and when she was done, she left to talk to Mr. Chuma and Mark, leaving Pamela next to her daughter. They then came back to talk to her mother, trying to find out the root of Ruthie's problem as she tried to advise them.

Ruthie woke up with a drip on her left arm and looked around, seeing that she was still in her room. Her mother and Mark were there talking to their family doctor. She tried to move her limbs but they were limp. She tried to talk but could not.

"Hey there girl, how are you feeling today?" her mother asked, walking towards her. Right on cue, their house girl walked in with some mashed potatoes mixed with bananas and some tomato soup, Ruthie's favorite meal when ill. Her mother helped her up and started feeding her. She pointed at some water, which her mother gave her. Her t-shirt hung loosely around her body. How many days was she out? She wondered. Her brother looked at her with so much pity in his eyes. She felt absolutely horrible. Her father walked into the room and went towards her, kissing her on the forehead. She ate half her food and finished off with some warm lemonade which her father had brought, and she felt much better. The doctor examined her once more and removed the line from her hand, then left a bandage in its place. She then asked for some time alone with Ruthie for an assessment, and her family left her room reluctantly.

"Your family is really worried about you, Ruthie. You passed out from crying so hard, according to your mother. You must be really stressed out. Is everything okay?" she asked, holding Ruthie's hand as she looked into her eyes with concern.

Ruthie felt fresh tears sting her eyes. "Do tear ducts rust? How much longer will this go on? I can't keep crying forever, can I? I just don't think I can remember how to not cry, it's a reflex," she said amid sobs.

The doctor rubbed her arm and replied, "Well you are really stressed out my dear, and the only way that I think this will end is by confronting what is making you feel this way. I am here to lend you my ear; perhaps I can help."

Ruthie narrated the events of that fateful afternoon and her history with Ethan. "The worst part is that I know that this isn't really about me but I cannot seem to stop crying. It took a lot for me to open up to someone else as much as I did with Ethan and I just don't know what to do anymore. I really thought everyone liked me. I put my very best foot forward and was the most modest person you've ever seen."

"Look here my dear, you are right, and none if this is your fault. Ethan seems to care about you a lot. Did you try asking him what happened on that day? Has he reached out?" the doctor asked.

She shook her head, "I switched off my phone because I don't want to seem desperate."

The doctor smiled at her, "I totally understand. You know, I had this boyfriend back in university; we were so in love with each other at first. We shared everything and could not imagine doing anything without each other. He was my rock," she narrated as she smiled fondly at her memories. "Then one time," she continued, "he decided to move into my house since it was in a better neighborhood and that was when things started falling apart. We felt like we had been sucked so much into each other's lives that we had lost sight of who we were and we had to go back to the drawing board and rediscover ourselves. We had to redefine our relationship and even move to a different house. We called that house a neutral ground for a fresh start. We talked about things and shared our lives before each other and decided to be naked and transparent with no secrets between us. When we did that, we embraced each other flaws and all, and do you know what happened to us after that? We got married and up to date, our family motto still remains. It's 'always tell the truth, no matter the consequences.'" She stated, "You never know; the truth always sets you free. Always. It is better to find a true and stable life and live it, than live a lie and end up losing your best life."

Ruthie had stopped crying and was now in deep thought. She had waited for those words all her life. She did not need to please and impress everyone. This was her life, *her* best life and she was missing out. She had promised herself to never let anyone affect her life this way. Looking at the doctor, she asked, "So what do you think? Should I start off by talking to my parents or to Ethan?"

"I don't know my dear, what do you feel is the easiest way? Who do you trust the most with this kind of information? Personally, I would trust your parents first, well, because of the whole family-versus-career thing, but you know best."

Ruthie smiled for the first time in three days. "Okay, I think I am ready to ask them."

The doctor called her parents in, and they were relieved to see her looking much better. The doctor then asked to leave, then smiled at Ruthie with reassurance. Mark walked her to the door to see her off.

"Okay mom, I'm sure dad told you about Ethan and what happened on that day. So please tell me, do you know a Nelly Amari?" his father was the first to freeze at the name and his jaw tightened a bit. Her mother seemed to think about it for a minute.

"That is Ethan's mom's name and when I mentioned your name, everything changed. Might you have handled one of her cases?"

Realization hit her suddenly, and she looked at her husband very briefly then at Ruthie. "Where did you say they lived again? Who else was there with you, and what exactly did they tell you?" she prompted. Right now, she was talking like a lawyer to her client more than a mother to her child. Her husband held her hand.

"Don't, please don't. She is not your client honey, she is our fragile daughter," he said as if signaling her about something.

"No, they did not tell me anything, they just asked who you were and cut the evening short. They were with a friend of hers, some white lady and her sons, around Ethan's age. Please tell me I am imagining you guys having your couple mental conversation. It's really annoying, you know." Her parents gave each other a knowing look then back at Ruthie.

"Well we knew each other long ago and have since lost touch; maybe there is still some bad blood. We had a horrible fallout. Have you talked to Ethan since? Are you two still dating?" her mother asked and her father seemed to be in deep thought.

"Mom, I said we were really close friends. We weren't dating but I was really considering him. He is one of the best guys I have ever met in my life."

"Well perhaps you should just leave it at that. We have history with his family and if they acted like that around you, then it seems you have your sign there. Let's leave it at that, you look tired," replied Pamela, puffing her pillows and avoiding her gaze. She was talking too fast. "Also, guess who was passing by this town and promised to be here tonight? Betty, the girl from your college. She mentioned having something in town and asked us to stay here for three days. She might be able to take your mind off things," her mother added with a guilty look on her face. "Wake up from there, take a shower and come meet us downstairs for some change in scenery, aunty wants to clean up your room anyway."

Ruthie got up from her bed and her sweats sagged low around her hips; she felt thin. After freshening up, she dressed up and switched on her phone. Immediately, Betty called her, stating that she was thirty minutes away. She could not help but think that something was amiss.

Betty's arrival was welcomed with a lot of unnecessary fuss and merriment as if there was some cover-up happening, but she went with it. She needed her own peace of mind in order to conduct her investigation soberly. Her brothers were more supportive than normal and her sisters seemed to act normal except for the fact that they did not do the bully her like normal. They played games and ate as they chatted away but when evening came, her parents locked themselves in the study and seemed to be discussing something serious. Her father even brought out his legal paraphernalia and reading glasses. They asked for their healthy juice: rosemary water with mint, lemons, and ginger that was sweetened with honey. Whenever this drink was made by the both of them, everyone in their household knew that it was about to go down. One could never even bother going in there. Her mother even put on her comfortable dungarees, which she only put on when she had a study research marathon. She could stay awake for close to fifty hours when dressed like that and she only took smoothie, coffee, and meal breaks. After, she would not talk to anyone until she was done freshening up and taking a strict six-hour sleep. Ruthie knew this was about her revelation but decided against telling anyone about it until she was sure she was on the right track.

After dinner, she went up to her room with Betty and she looked for her keys to lock the door, which she could not find. They always confiscated her keys whenever she had one of her episodes. "Mark!" she called angrily as she headed to her brother's room. "Did you take the keys to my room? Seriously I have a guest over and we need to have our private time!" she shouted at her brother who kept looking at his phone without even acknowledging her. "Mark! You are the worst!"

"Go talk to your parents with that nasty attitude; they have your keys," he said nonchalantly. She knew she could not go there, especially at this time. She went back to her room and slammed her door. Then she pushed her dressing table against the door, locking it. Betty was lying on her bed just observing her.

"Should I be worried? Calm down, I brought some of my special brownies and wine." She winked at her, reaching for her backpack. Ruthie could really use some of that. They had to drink wine directly from the bottle as she could not go for glasses from the kitchen; there was a strict policy in their house forbidding whatever they were up to. "So talk to me girl, whose funeral are we planning?" Betty started after a few sips. Ruthie narrated to her friend the whole story, plus her parents' reaction and the entire vibe of the house afterwards. Something was definitely amiss as Betty agreed.

"What about Ethan? Have you talked to him yet? Do you think he knows something?" she asked.

"Well when I switched on my phone, I found that he had tried calling me, but I did not bother calling back. I am not ready to read his texts yet. I only saw one where he had apologized but it was vague. I can't deal with that right now. Whatever it is, he is involved."

They went online and did some thorough research on her parents' cases that involved single mothers, custody battles and even community women in their small town and came up with nothing. She looked up Ethan's biological father's name in various combinations but it was futile. They only found dirt on exes and other friends and soon drifted to gossip.

"What do you think this is about?" Betty asked with real fatigue in her eyes. Ruthie felt defeated. She thought about sneaking into her parents' study room but knew they were not going to sleep until they finished whatever top-secret project they were working on, and even if they were not in the room, everything would be under lock and key, or even in the safe. "Whatever happened to Cedric? You are too proud, mama, he was the best match for you. Remember how he ensured your recovery that one time?" Betty asked, going through Cedric's social media profile. He had a child and a serious girlfriend who he was planning a wedding with.

"Well, he saw me at my ugliest and was present during a time that I was not ready to settle again. Frankly, I think he was scared that I would do him dirty like that other scumbag." They both laughed at that. "Actually, I'm surprised that you stayed after witnessing my crazy," she added.

"Oh, girl, I have my fair share of crazy, and we both know I could take you if you tried anything like that on me." They giggled, remembering the day they fought over a dress when they lived together. It ended up in pieces after that and they both took some wine and exchanged makeup as a peace offering.

They gossiped and stalked for a while and then decided to sleep. Ruthie heard her phone ring insistently and Betty slapped her. "Put it on silent or pick the damn phone." She woke up and saw that it was Ethan calling. She put her phone on silent and went back to bed. Then Betty's phone started ringing.

"God! What have we done to deserve this?" she asked, reaching for her phone, not even bothering to check the caller identity.

"Hello?"

"Hi Betty, it's Ethan, Ruthie's uuh, friend. Have you heard from her?" came the voice on the other side. She woke up fully, hitting Ruthie insistently.

"Ouch!" Ruthie complained.

"Please hold, can I call you back in a few?" she asked and hung up, not even bothering to wait for the response. "You won't believe who called me. It's Ethan. He wants to know whether you are alive."

"Oh shit! What do we do now? Should we ask him?" Ruthie was so conflicted. She went to the bathroom and freshened up while Betty put her room in order as she waited for her turn. "I will read his messages first before we decide. What do you think?" Ruthie said as she applied oil on herself. "Go freshen up while I go check for some breakfast then we will come back and see what's up."

She dressed fast as Betty freshened up before joining her in the dining room. Her brothers seemed to be in a deep discussion in the living room and were looking at some document, talking in low tones. They saw Ruthie and put it down. "Morning sunshine, where is your BFF, your lifeline, your-" Jabari started.

"Oh, shut up! I don't care what you guys are doing, just stay out of my business," she snapped as she took a huge gulp of some refreshing passionfruit juice. As if on cue, Betty joined her and finished hers in one gulp as well.

"Tough night, huh? Should we go up and share in your merriment? Don't be selfish." The girls ignored them and served themselves a heavy breakfast, then went back to Ruthie's room. Ethan's texts were filled with "His" and "sorry" and a lot of "I can explain but talk to your parents first."

"What do you think Mark and Jabari were hiding? I saw them with something and they were speaking in low tones." Ruthie asked Betty.

"Do you think it's a piece of the puzzle?"

"I have to get my hands on that document. But first, let's call Ethan and see what he knows."

Betty called Ethan back and put it on speaker. "Hello? I'm so sorry to call you like this but Ruthie has not been picking my calls or answering my texts. I really need to talk to her."

"Gee, I wonder why," Betty said sarcastically.

"Listen Betty, I know it has been a hard four days but you have to understand, I didn't know about it myself, up until that day. Well, I knew, I just did not connect the dots up until she said who her parents are. You have to trust me Betty, I seriously would have approached this whole thing differently."

Betty and Ruthie looked at each other in shock.

"Okay, how else would you have approached it?" Betty asked cautiously, indirectly seeking as much information as she could.

"I don't know, I would have prepared her, and even my family, we would have not met the way we did and maybe we would have talked to our parents about it first, you know, maturely, and allowed all us time to let everything sink in. I can't believe how small this world is. Please tell her that if we do it together it's going to be easier. I'm sure her parents have forbidden any contact with me, but please talk to her. I will always be here and I am ready to meet up for discussion."

"Well I will talk to her about it, then we can see what to do, though I cannot promise anything." She hung up. Well, this was much more complicated than they thought.

"Hear me out. What if we pretend to have the information and trick Ethan into spilling it? How about that?" Betty asked. Ruthie was still in deep thought.

"Clearly we won't learn anything from my parents, and I think my brothers are in on it too. So annoying. Let me set up a meeting and we will let him spill it. I won't take no for an answer. I hate being in the dark this much." She headed to her closet. "This calls for a celebration. We are one step away to our big victory." She pulled out a bottle of whiskey that was hidden under her clothes, deep into her closet. It was almost halfway empty. Betty could not believe her eyes.

"You made us drink that cheap crap when you've had this all along? How long have you been hiding it?" she asked, taking a long swig, then contorted her face as she swallowed and passed it to Ruthie.

"Well I have my secrets too." They took turns until they were so drunk that they started shouting and laughing. They went downstairs, still in a good mood, and found her siblings watching a movie.

"Look who is in a good mood. Come on, share with us or we will tell mom," Mark said.

"Well we will share our secrets if you share yours, if not leave us, leave us. Wow I sound so grown up; stay away from our secrets," she said, laughing and stuttering and then "high-fived" with Betty.

"Alrighty then, we will buy our own and don't even bother asking to borrow from us," Jabari said, taking out his phone.

"Shush please don't, we will share ours and you will buy us some more, then we can all be one happy drinking family," she whispered loudly and everyone laughed.

"Go back to your room and the girls will bring up some food-" he directed.

"And some fresh cold juice," Ruthie interrupted. "Yes, and some fresh cold juice for you two, then we will talk about the drinking family." They hurried upstairs and continued laughing and gossiping. When their food arrived, they wolfed it down and blacked out. They woke up when it was dark outside and found everyone having dinner except, of course, Ruthie's parents.

"Your parents sure know how to bury themselves in work. When will they come out to and see the light?" Betty asked as they sat at the table.

"Right now, actually. We are famished and have missed our family. Hello everyone." Ruthie's mother entered with a smile and a pot in her hands with their father close by, smiling brightly, just as they always did after a successful day at work. They all responded and soon enough they were eating and drinking and laughing. They acted as if the previous days had not happened.

"I hear we might have to take you two for rehab if you continue with whatever you've been doing," her mother said, addressing Ruthie and Betty. "No one told on you, everything that happens under this roof is well known to us. Keep it on the minimum next time, and of course we will not condone that kind of drinking here. All drinks should be kept in the bar and the drinking should be monitored, understood?"

"Yes ma'am, we apologize."

"Good, now what's new in Betty's world? I have been dying to try out her lasagna again. Will you bless us with it tomorrow? I can't for the love of me make it the way you do despite following your recipe step by step," Ruthie's mother said.

"Well the secret ingredient is Betty's love; you can't buy that anywhere. I will be honored, Mrs. Chuma," she stated with a lot of pride. She loved it when people commended her food. She had dreamed of opening her own restaurant with various dishes tweaked to perfection. She had rejected offers of opening a substandard restaurant that did not fully capture her dream restaurant. Frankly, she would much rather open a food truck business as she could make it her own. Right now, she worked as a temporary assistant at a financial institution just to pay her bills. They finished eating and everyone retired to their rooms.

The next day, their parents woke up early and left without a word; Ruthie's father had his briefcase and their mother her business suit. It was weird, considering that none of them had worked this hard on anything in a long time. Ruthie texted Ethan, asking for a date and location to discuss matters.

Ethan responded immediately. *"Thanks a lot, we can meet tomorrow. Go to Valley chips at eleven."* She did not even bother responding as she had to do some power play. They spent their afternoon deciding on their outfits, put their makeup on, and took photos for The Gram. Her parents arrived at around nine in the evening, looking tired and defeated; her mother's eyes were a little bit teary. They went straight to their room, leaving everyone puzzled.

Mark and Jabari gave each other some perplexed looks, then retreated to Jabari's room. The mood was so tense that Ruthie could not wait to talk to Ethan. Whatever the problem was, it went deeper than they had imagined. Betty tried talking to the twins but they seemed as clueless as the two girls were. She then decided to take a different approach.

"Follow my lead, Ruthie." They went to Jabari's room where the boys were and knocked

"It has been so tense here, can we at least go for a game out in the court?" Betty asked politely. Mark looked up at the girls and then at Jabari.

"Sure, just give us a few minutes, we have to finish up with something." When they had gone to change into sportswear up in Ruthie's room, she asked her friend.

"Okay, you know very well that I don't play, especially with you and my brothers. What's up?"

"It's a good distraction for one and two, their room will be open and you will finally get to see whatever is in that document they are hiding. You will use your feeble bones or something as an excuse to get back to the house while we play."

They dressed hurriedly and were soon joined by the boys.

"How do you want to do this?" Mark asked as he stretched.

"Mark and I versus you two," said Ruthie as Mark groaned in disapproval. Ruthie was too clueless about the game. She made so many mistakes which really affected the flow of the game; Ruthie got mad as everyone kept blaming her for it and Betty suggested that she go to the house while they played a real game. She threw the ball angrily and stomped off, secretly glad that she had finally gotten her chance.

She went straight to Jabari's room and went through his desk, then opened his drawers- therein lied the coveted document. It was DNA results. Mark Chuma and Jabari Chuma, no match. *What does this mean?* She wondered.

She then put the document back and knew that the document was part of the story. She went and freshened up until Betty joined her and she revealed the new piece of information.

"We need to get more of it. What is the connection with Ethan's family, though?" they debated.

The next morning, their parents had breakfast in bed. Ruthie and Betty dressed up to meet Ethan but resolved not to let anyone know about it.

"Where are we headed today, ladies?" Mark asked.

"Town. We figured we need some change in environment. Does anyone need anything?" Ruthie responded.

"Where in town will you be?" Mark asked. "I need to pick up a mug for my fiancé at Baraka Mall, would you do the honors? Her birthday is coming up and I can't think of a gift. While you are at it, pick something you think she would love. Here is my card, don't abuse it. No alcohol, drugs, or anything above two thousand shillings for you two, okay?"

They nodded happily and took the card, then left.

"And no meeting up with boys!" Jabari shouted back at them as they left the gate.

CHAPTER FIVE

The Truth Comes Out

ETHAN HAD WOKEN UP EARLY that morning and debated whether or not to still meet up with Ruthie. He was going to have to hide from his mother and nosy sister. He was relieved to find out that their date was still on despite the previous day's events—Ethan could not believe her parent's guts, coming to their home with documents and threats without any basis. He thought about the events that had happened.

He heard a knock on the door and when he opened it, he saw Mr. and Mrs. Chuma with a heavy briefcase and stern faces. He noticed that Mrs. Chuma had an unsure look in her eyes.

"Yes, may I help you?" he asked with a sneer.

"We are here for your mother. Can we come in?" answered Mrs. Chuma.

"What is this about, if I may ask?" asked Ethan as his mother shouted from the kitchen.

"Who is it?"

"Nelly, we are here to talk about something that I'm sure you are well aware of," said Mr. Chuma, loud enough from the door for his mom to hear her. Ms. Amari recognized the voice and she felt her stomach churn. She felt a wave of dizziness, then sat down, breathing in and out slowly as she tried to compose herself. She drank two full glasses of water and went to the living room, finding her son and the uninvited guests in a staring contest.

"What are you waiting for Ethan? Invite them in," said Ms. Amari.

Ethan moved from the door and went up to his room. He heard them talk in low tones and the shuffle of papers.

"Ethan! Come here for a moment please!" his mother called from the room.

He walked to the living room. "Yes, what is it?" he asked.

"Well, you are required to sign these documents, forbidding you from talking to Ruthie, meeting with her, or telling her about our history. I'm sure you know why," Mrs. Chuma said, handing over a pen and the documents to Ethan.

"Why exactly would I do that? We are not related in any way. I am not party to your business and I have the right to choose my friends."

"Please Ethan, don't make this harder than it already is. We have lived peacefully so far because we complied. Fighting these two will just do us more harm than good," pleaded Ms. Amari.

"I am not fighting anyone. Ms. Elgah has done her best to raise her sons alone over the years, I have seen you two struggle, ma. Pamela here is a mother and she works with other struggling mothers. She knows she has made them suffer and the degree of it. Haven't we all suffered enough because of them? Also, what do I have to do with it?" he asked in anger.

"Please it's best if we keep quiet and comply," prompted his mother.

"I'm not signing anything. Please, take me to court and I will spill everything I know. Do you even know what your own daughter has been through? I talk to her more than you do. So, if you need to protect her, go talk to her in private and sort out your family issues. Leave ours alone."

"Watch how you speak about my family, boy!" said Mr. Chuma angrily. His wife had a confused look on her face.

"Why are you so determined to go all these lengths to keep something like this from them? What will they do if they know they have other siblings? We have no desire to tell your family anything and I am pretty sure you've seen that everything has been running fine, even without you. We had even forgotten you existed."

"Ethan please, just do as they say so that they can leave," Ms. Amari begged.

"Mom, for how long will you cower? These people have nothing on us. What will they sue us for? For revealing the truth? Making them take responsibility for their actions? Please sue me, I'm not signing anything. I'm not party to this suit. And when I am served with any court document, the whole world will have a new juicy story trending. And I will say everything. Everything. So please leave now before I sue you for trespassing."

Mrs. Chuma started sobbing and Mr. Chuma's eyes were red with anger. He started shaking.

"Let's go. We will sort this out later. Let's not do something that will tear everything down," said Pamela, holding her husband's shaking hand as if to calm him. They stood up and left.

Ethan was still unsure whether he was going to meet Ruthie, since she didn't reply to his text to confirm the meeting anyway. He dressed up casually and even put on sandals so as not to raise alarm, then he told his mother that he was going for a little stroll to clear his mind.

"Don't do anything stupid. I have been at peace for so long; choose your battles wisely, son."

He left for town and went straight to Valley Chips. He arrived thirty minutes early and sat at a dark corner where he could spot anyone coming in. He ordered a cup of coffee and requested the Wi-Fi password then scrolled through his phone, occasionally looking up until he spotted Ruthie and Betty walking in. Ethan was sweating profusely. He wiped his hands at the sides of his jeans and stood up. They greeted each other and everyone sat nervously. They were still waiting in awkward silence when the waiter came and took the girl's orders.

"I didn't think you would show. Do your parents know where you are?" he asked.

"No, they don't know yet. I didn't think you would show up either," she responded.

"So I assume you know about your parents' visit then. I had to clear the air before taking the coward's way. I signed nothing though, so don't worry, I won't be going to jail." Betty and Ruthie looked at each other in wonder.

"But your mom and sister signed?" Ruthie asked, still not sure what was happening.

"No, my sister is not yet eighteen so my mom signed it for her as her guardian. I seriously don't know why we are doing all this." Ethan started feeling annoyed and frustrated as the girls just sipped their drinks. "We are not related. I mean, maybe my mother made a bad call back in the day, threatening your father, but really, where does my family come into play with this? I really like you and care about you, and I want you in my life. We should just come out and lay everything in the open. It really is not our fault that happened."

Betty felt like she was in the middle of a Romeo and Juliet story, in every aspect possible.

"I care about you too, Ethan, but now what are we going to do?" Ruthie asked.

"This involves Ms. Vaughn and your parents. Frankly, we are only involved due to the fact that my mother was helping her try to beat your father in court, and the threats she tried sending your parents back then, but what does that matter now?" Ethan responded, creasing his forehead.

"What does Ms. Vaughn have anything to do with this?" Ruthie asked.

Ethan froze. "You didn't know? Oh my God! What have your parents told you?"

"What does Ms. Vaughn have to do with this?" Ruthie asked again, firmly.

"Okay we know nothing, that's why we are here. Spill, or else," Betty butted in.

Ethan ran his hand over his face as his heartbeat accelerated. He was sweating and confused. "Why, what do you know? What did you think this was about?" he asked nervously, seriously considering dashing out in one quick sprint and going home to rethink his choices.

"Spill it boy! We don't have all day," Betty snapped.

"Okay, Jack and Derrick are your half-brothers."

"What?" Betty and Ruthie both said in unison.

"I promise I didn't realize the connection up until the whole fiasco at dinner. I swear to God." Ethan finished raising his hands in surrender.

"What exactly are you saying?" Ruthie asked, suddenly feeling a wave of dizziness.

"Your father was with Ms. Vaughn, then they had a falling out."

"I'm pretty sure we know what a half-brother means. Tell us the full story," Betty snapped as Ruthie's eyes grew red in anger. Her heart was pounding so wildly that her top moved along with it. Was she hearing all of it wrong?

"Wait a minute. Mark is older than the twins and so is Jabari. What are you telling us right now?" Ruthie asked.

"Well, all I know is that your dad was with Ms. Vaughn for some time and she fell into a depression and had a tubal litigation. There were some cultural complications as well as legal battles, which were fought by both your parents who, by the way, were unstoppable back in the day. Apparently, your parents were together as well and the whispered story is that they could not coexist with Mama Jack, so the whole thing was put away and we never heard about it again. I actually thought your parents moved to another town."

Ruthie felt a wave of nausea and rushed to the washroom, followed closely by Betty who was also in grave shock.

"What the hell?" Betty said in the washroom. "What the *actual* hell?" She kept saying it over and over again, as Ruthie vomited her guts out until her knees gave way. Betty went and helped her up and then they cleaned up, silently looking in the mirror at each other, then at themselves. Betty gave her a tight bear hug.

"She is a lovely woman, Betty. She held me tight and we caught up with them. Really, they are a lovely, lovely family. And the twins, oh my God, the twins are just, well they are so brotherly and accepting. I can't believe this," Ruthie said, still holding tight onto Betty as if her life depended on it. She didn't want to let go.

"Everything okay in there? Is everyone decent? I'm coming in," Ethan said as he cautiously entered the ladies' room with one palm over his eyes, making the girls break their embrace as they giggled. He sure did know how to lighten the mood. He stopped at the entrance, looking over his shoulder. "Please come out, I am getting worried."

They followed him back to the table, finding that he had ordered a round of Ruthie's favorite lemonade for the three of them.

"Ethan, I am so sorry. I didn't know about all this. You must think I'm from a horrible family. I swear I also didn't know. What documents did they bring over for you to sign? Haven't they done enough already?" Ruthie asked after settling down in her seat and taking a sip of her drink.

"Don't worry, it's not your fault, has never been, and will never be. They brought over more non-disclosure agreements and other documents. I hear they also brought some money, which both Ms. Vaughn and my mother rejected. But they signed the documents. Your mother seems like a not-so-bad person, but she can be fierce. Why do they still want this under wraps? Isn't your dad retired already?" he asked her.

"That's what I want to know. Then there is this whole age thing that I want to know about. I can't believe the twins are my brothers," replied Ruthie as Betty kept searching for something online.

"Oh, my goodness! Your dad is really thorough," Betty spoke up. "I have checked all Kenya law reports, every custody battle, even entered their initials and found nothing. Where exactly did they bury the legal battles?"

They talked and talked until Ruthie's phone rang. It was her brother.

"Where are you guys? Did you find anything nice for her?" he asked.

"For who?" Ruthie responded absentmindedly.

"You forgot about the main thing that took you to town? Where are you?" he barked.

"Oh! Calm down, we met with one of Betty's old classmates in town and she took us out for lunch and lost track of time. I'm sorry, we are headed there right now." She hung up. They paid the bills and left for the mall with Ethan. The mood had lightened and the shopping was a happy distraction.

"So, what next? I feel like we need to tell my father that we know the truth. I bet Mark and Jabari know already."

"Poor Ms. Elgah and her children. What can we do to make this better?" said Betty.

"Well, they've made it this far. I just need to have the freedom to date you, interact with whoever I want and free my parents and aunt Elgah from those contracts."

"Well we need to find all information we need, from both sides. Then we can meet and compare notes."

"What do we do from there? All that information and for what? How will that free my mom?" Ethan asked.

"Depending on the information we gather, we will figure it out from there. We have to play this perfectly. We only have one shot," Ruthie responded.

It was finally time to go home and Ruthie had decided to open herself to taking her relationship with Ethan further- a more serious level. He was home to her. They said their goodbyes and went their separate ways.

When they arrived at the gate, Ruthie stopped, breathed in, and out and decided to play this one slowly. She told Betty to act normal and try her best to ignore whatever weird vibes would go on in the house. As soon as she opened the gate, her brothers came out to greet them.

"Okay, this is new. I didn't bring you guys anything except what you asked me to, so save your hugs for a more relevant person." She dodged her brothers' embraces and they ended up knocking their heads together, making Betty laugh. She went and started unpacking in the sitting room, revealing matching bracelets for her sisters, two necklaces for herself and Betty, and a pair of happy socks each for her brothers. She then revealed a big wrapped gift box and handed it over to her brother.

"This is for her, from me, and this," she said revealing a smaller box, "is the pathetic mug you got for her. Don't worry, I added a thoughtful chain with a locket inside that has matching earrings. You're welcome."

"Hmm, nothing in there for us?" her mother budged in.

"Too bad we only gave her life, maybe she would have gotten us something if we had done something bigger, huh?" her father added, and they all laughed.

"Well, as for you," Ruthie replied, "I will get you something once I start earning my own money, or would you prefer using your cash for your own gifts? Plus, you took away my keys, so." she said as she went up to her room, followed by Betty.

"Sorry for ensuring your safety, baby!" her mother shouted back at her.

Once in Ruthie's room, Betty released a huge exhale and threw herself on the bed. "This is like reality television. I don't even know how to keep up any more. Whew! I'm so glad you're in my life, otherwise I would be bored to death."

Ruthie fiddled with the promise ring that Ethan had already gotten her at the mall; it started as a joke but he ended up getting it for her as a promise to stay true to her and stand by her during the drama until everyone's lives went back to normal. *He was so sweet*, she smiled fondly at her reflection.

There was a knock at their door; it was Jabari. "Please Betty, come play some basketball with us. Ruthie has been hogging you the entire time and we need some challenges here. Mark is getting all rusty." Betty beamed at that. She had not played in a long time and enjoyed playing with Ruthie's brothers; they had no mercy for her, which made it much more fun for her.

"Sounds good! Someone here is off in their own world and I could use the break. Let me change into something more comfortable. I will be there in a minute." She jumped towards Ruthie's closet for some sweats and t-shirt. She always had her comfortable shoes with her. Ruthie hung back and chatted with Ethan until dinner time, when a sweaty Betty walked into her room, looking tired but refreshed. She walked to the shower as Ruthie made her way to the dining room.

"Betty and I will be making tomorrow's meals- well just breakfast and lunch. Yes, it will be the lasagna mom. She said she will leave tomorrow after lunch," Ruthie explained as she served herself.

"Alright baby girl," her father responded.

Everyone later joined in for dinner and they had some catching up to do. Betty expressed her gratitude to Ruthie's family and promised to come back soon. Ruthie's mother still offered her a research job at her organization which she politely declined for the millionth time.

"You hate your job anyway, why not be close to your people? You are family now. Plus you would be living rent-free," she added.

Ruthie could not believe her ears; her mother pretending to be all hospitable, motherly and accommodating while she made two boys live in misery and dragged down an extra family in the process.

"I'm sorry, but no. My savings are getting somewhere, and I am this close to opening "Betty's Finest Restaurant," where you will all get family discounts." She gestured as her eyes lit up as they did when she talked about her restaurant.

"Ruthie, are you okay? Why the long face; do you really hate restaurants that much?" her father asked.

"No, I just thought of something really nasty. Lost my appetite," she responded, rising to take her plate to the kitchen. She came back with well-sliced pineapples and placed them at the center of the dining table before sitting down to eat.

"I hear we should prepare our stomachs for your amazing cooking, Betty," her mother continued. Betty had noticed Ruthie's leg shaking under the table, and she decided to carry the conversation and create as much distraction as she could. She talked about cooking, sports, and even her family back home, then excused herself, claiming that amazing chefs had to get their beauty sleep. Ruthie agreed.

"Ruthie isn't even a chef, she is just the story teller who stays on her phone while you're cooking," dissed Jabari.

"You are not even-" Ruthie started before being interrupted by Betty.

"Well I will make sure we leave our phones upstairs. Let's go; as much as I wanted to hear that comeback, I think sleep is more important," she said, signaling for Ruthie not to explode. She knew Ruthie was about to spill the beans and spoil everything. When they were behind closed doors, Betty admonished her, "So madam DNA, were you about to say he is not even your brother? Do we know that story? Please control yourself. I know it's hard considering the fact that this is your family and not just the sick psycho you practiced your FBI skills on, but you need to do this right. I will try to gather as much information, as should you. I'm pretty sure Ethan is also trying to gain information as well."

Ruthie sighed and plopped on her bed. "I just felt like calling her on her hospitality bullshit. Why does she feel the need to pretend to be all motherly and looking out for women when deep down she knows what she did to Vaughn and her sons? God, I hate her guts!" she responded.

"Let's just get our facts right before we do this. Okay? Promise me." They made their promises and Betty took out their last pot brownie to share as planned. Soon enough, they drifted off to sleep.

The next morning, they woke up bright and early and prepared a heavy breakfast of mixed baked nuts, samosas, pancakes and African Betty's finest tea, as she called it. They also made French toast, an assortment of fruits, and freshly-squeezed mixed fruit juice. They set the table as Betty prescribed. She really loved Ruthie's house; her mother was a hoarder and had all sorts of fancy things, from the kitchen utensils to table décor, and she used them to the maximum.

"Mmmhh, what smells great in here? Oh my goodness. Hey! You guys, come quickly and see this!" her mother shouted, and soon enough everyone came rushing to the dining room. It looked heavenly.

"If I wasn't already engaged, I would propose to you right now."

"Please come live with us."

"That's it, we are firing aunty."

"Is this how you ate while living with her, Ruthie?"

"How are you so talented at everything?"

"Do you not eat what you cook? How are you not fat?"

Everyone was talking at once. Nobody moved to touch the table. Mrs. Chuma rushed to her bedroom for her camera and took multiple photos. She always did for every dish Betty made, stating that she could use them when the time came to open her restaurant. She then asked the whole family to gather around the table with Betty in the middle for a photo. More clicks came and went until everyone got tired and dug in. The meal was heavenly; it surpassed everyone's imagination. The boys even offered to clean the dishes.

Everyone retired to the living room where they started watching a movie, when Ruthie's parents came in with a package. "This is for you, Betty. We wanted to give it to you when you opened your restaurant but after this morning's meal, we could not wait to hand it over. It's a little something to get you started on your career."

She opened it with eagerness as everyone looked curiously. It was a set of professional chef's knives from Japan, two aprons each with a B on them and a chef's hat and shirt. When she opened up the shirt, two oven mittens dropped on her lap; they each had a B on them as well. She felt tears well up her eyes and rushed to hug them. She could not believe her luck. This was the best present anyone had given to her.

"Much as we would love to take all the credit, everyone chipped in a little," Mrs. Chuma said as she wiped her own tears.

"Oh my goodness, Ruthie, how long have you kept this from me? This is too much. I really want to say I can't take it but I am afraid if I do, you might take it all back and I really love every one of them. Thanks a lot, you guys. You didn't have to," she said amid tears. This was her second family. It made her feel bad that she was going behind their backs, carrying on with the "investigation." Ruthie even forgot all about it for a moment. She loved Betty like a sister and wanted all good things for her; she couldn't ruin her friend's moment. Those items were a startup to her culinary career. Betty's happy smile was much more than she could bear.

Betty video-called her parents and siblings, showcasing her new equipment as they greeted the Chumas, thanking them. She went up to Ruthie's room and safely packed her gifts, then called Ruthie to the kitchen to make the best Lasagna she had ever prepared. She even made two extra ones and stored them in the freezer as a surprise thank you, and told Ruthie to only show it to them when she had already left. She then made some chocolate mousse as dessert and some fruit salad.

After the heavenly lunch, her parents, Ruthie, and the twins took Betty to town to bid her goodbye, then went back home. Ruthie went to her room and called Ethan, asking if he had gathered any more information, then compared notes and planned to meet in a few days. They were all three like secret agents. They talked in secret and stole documents, snooped on text messages, and even took pictures of document copies. Betty's work was minimal as she entirely depended on the internet for information, although she did help in piecing together the information acquired and provided them with new ideas.

Soon it was the meeting day. Betty had travelled again all the way but had not yet arrived at Ruthie's home; they had to meet in town first. They compared notes and decided on the angle to approach the matter.

It was the last week of their holiday and they knew that they needed to act fast. Whatever was going down, it was to happen during that weekend. They had to trick three families into meeting and if they played it wrongly, it would blow up in their faces. They also had to choose a private location due to the sensitivity and severity of the matter. They pooled their resources together and came up with a master plan.

Ruthie arrived at home with Betty and everyone was in the sitting room. "Look who I found in town you guys! Cancel all your plans tomorrow because we have a surprise for you!" she shouted excitedly, attracting everyone's attention. They all welcomed her and after the greetings, she continued, "She got us a reservation at *Maendeleo* Resort for the entire afternoon, and in our own comfortable private area. We could all go and have one final outing there before we all resume our busy schedules. Sound good?" She looked at everyone with pleading eyes. Nobody could deny her that one request. They all agreed to free their afternoon and leave at around noon.

They ran up to her room so that nobody could see their nervousness. They agreed to carry all their stuff in Betty's backpack as no one would suspect anything. She texted Ethan who took too long to respond, but they could not risk calling him and blow the entire operation.

When Ethan got home, he went straight to the bathroom to freshen up, then went and found his mother and Molly in the kitchen. "Hi guys, how was your day?"

"It was okay," responded Molly as their mother tried her best to ignore her son.

"Mom, how are you?" he asked cautiously, ready for her to explode.

"Ethan, what you did was wrong, it was risky and I am still very scared and annoyed with you. Do you know who these people are?" she asked angrily.

"Mom, I said I'm sorry. I will not repeat that and if they come again, I will sign whatever they want, okay?" he responded too fast. His mother looked at him suspiciously. Her son was not one to give up and change his mind so quickly.

"Did they get to you?" she asked.

"No, I just realized that family is more important," he responded looking down. "Is dinner ready; can I start setting the table?" he tried changing the subject.

"Ethan, something is up and I will get to the bottom of this. I hope you know what you are getting yourself into," his mother responded suspiciously.

"Mom I said nothing is up, I just cleared my mind and thought about what I did, okay?" he responded, raising his voice a bit to mask his anxiety. He then turned and went up to his room.

When dinner was ready, Molly called him down. He reluctantly went to the dining room and sat quietly.

"Dear Lord, thank you for this meal, we pray that you may bless it as we partake in it. We also pray for Ethan; may he find his way and may you give him your wisdom. He needs it. Shine him with your brightest of lights to guide his way because he seems to be blind nowadays. Above all give us peace. Amen." Their mother prayed without acknowledging anyone and started serving. Everyone ate in silence. When the meal was almost over, he spoke up.

"Mom, I am really sorry for how I acted. To show you how much, I booked the suite at *Maendeleo* Resort for tomorrow afternoon. It was an offer I saw and decided we could spend the afternoon there with Ms. Vaughn and the boys, to just forget what happened and have some fun; is that okay?"

"Well we were to meet up with the Vaughns tomorrow, and this whole mess is partly your fault, so yes, we'll take it. Don't spring any more surprises on us, okay?" Ms. Amari responded.

Ethan agreed nervously as he cleared the table and left for his room. He questioned their plan again and almost called Ruthie to call off the entire mission, but decided against it. He then called Derrick who needed no convincing, so long as there was food.

'We are on for twelve thirty. Remember to pray about all this," he texted Ruthie. Everyone was so extremely tensed out that Betty could not even bring herself to use any mind-altering substances. It was hard for all of them. Betty and Ruthie tried watching a comedy, thriller, and even their favorite video mixtapes but they could not focus. They decided to go out back and work out in the dark, which gave them the ability to blow off some steam by smoking a joint. Then they went to sleep, not even bothering to shower.

The next day they woke up bright and early and went for a jog. Then they freshened up and went to help the twins with their hair and makeup as a distraction. Her parents had woken up early as well and were catching up on the latest politics as they sipped their teas and discussed them. Her brothers were just the normal annoying people they usually were; when it was almost eleven, they were still playing basketball. They then went inside after Ruthie's cries and decided to play Fifa- Ruthie was almost crying as she begged them to get ready. Eventually they got ready and went their way, the girls with the parents and the men in Mark's car. Betty wanted to ride with the men, but Ruthie refused, claiming that she was not in a mood to be all friendly with them.

When they arrived, she was a nervous wreck. They were shown to their private area and sat down and ordered for drinks as they browsed the menu.

"This place is so spacious; such a waste that Betty's family is not close by. We would have all fit here comfortably," Mr. Chuma started.

Ruthie kept looking at the entrance of their area nervously until she saw Ethan's family walk in. Nobody noticed each other except the planners until Ms. Vaughn gasped loudly.

"Oh my Goodness Ethan! What the hell?" the whole room froze as Ruthie stood up.

"No, it's me, don't blame Ethan."

Derrick and Jack said "oh hell no!" in unison as they attempted to exit the room.

"No please Jack, Derrick, please stay. We found something that we think should be addressed."

"Ethan what did you do, boy?" his mother pleaded, almost crying.

"Ruthie, whatever you think you found, you did not, what is wrong with you?" her father asked firmly. Betty had gone to shut the door of their area and told the waiters that she would call them to get their orders.

"Please let's all sit down and hear us out." Ruthie's sisters were at a loss while her brothers just looked down and talked in whispers, and her mother started wiping tears. Ruthie herself was close to tears as her voice broke while she talked.

Molly was right behind her mother. "Mom, please sit down. We can sit separately for now because we understand the tension, but please sit somewhere."

They sat so far apart and everyone was emotional. Ethan's mother looked scared for her life.

CHAPTER SIX

Ripping Off the Band Aid

"Everyone hates change, but sometimes ripping off the band aid is the best way forward"

BETTY OPENED THE DOOR AND called in the waiter who took their drink orders then left and shut the door. Everyone remained silent; there was a lot of tension and everyone could hear their own heartbeats. Her father was in deep thought and her mother was still sobbing. Jack and Derrick were in a mood to kill while Betty, Ethan, and Ruthie were sitting in between them all, all too nervous to even talk. The waiter came in with the drinks and said he would come for their meal orders as soon as they wanted, then he left, shutting the door behind him.

"So, are we going to be told why we have been summoned? What's your angle here, Ruthie?" Mr. Chuma started.

"Take it easy, let's hear her out," Mark responded.

"Okay, as we now all know, I decided to date Ethan, but we have a lot of family, er, differences. We wish to address them, and not only for the sake of our relationship, but also for the transparency of everything. I believe we have been living a lie for so many years and having interacted with all of you separately, I seriously think it's time to just live and put everything on the table." Ruthie paused as Ethan's mother started crying and Molly was rubbing her back with teary eyes as well.

"We understand that this will open up some old wounds, and we are young and probably stupid, but this issue has been going on long enough," Ethan continued. "I don't think that it's necessary to keep living with all this bad blood. I apologize for all this to all of you, but we can agree that it will set all of us free."

"Yes. You are young, and you should not have meddled in our affairs. These are things that you would never understand. I think I'm speaking for all the adults here when I say we should just leave things the way they are," Mr. Chuma said sternly as he gave Ruthie a look he only gave problematic prosecutors and advocates in court. She had dreaded being on the other side of the look and it made her shudder.

"Dad, please, this is already out, and I think it's time we talked about it," Jabari answered his father in a collected and sober tone. "Mark and I also need to get some things off our chests as well as Jack and Derrick, I presume. Moreover, talking about it will be much easier for everyone in the long run. We can also come up with a dynamic."

Ms. Vaughn was wearing a scowl the whole time that would occasionally turn to sadness, pity, then the scowl again. Betty wondered what had been going on in her mind.

"Ethan and I would have snuck around and waited until we were back in the city and have our affair, but we decided against it. The bigger picture dictates that secrets, lies, and sneaking around is what brought us here. We cannot go on like this; you all are wonderful people."

Her mother was now sobbing uncontrollably and so was Ethan's mother. The rest of the party was filled with scowls and pity. Betty left the room and came back with an assortment of cocktails and tissues which she distributed. She went and soothed Ruthie's mother and the room now became attentive. Everyone was sipping their cocktails.

"Okay, we discovered that we have half-brothers, Derrick and Jack, and we also found this paper here. These are DNA results that Mark and Jabari took behind everybody's back. It seems they also made their own discoveries. I am sorry again for snooping but it was meant to happen. I mean, I must have met Ethan for a reason," Ruthie started as their father shot a look at Mark. Mark took a long gulp of his cocktail.

"I would much rather unpack Mark's baggage first before anyone else. I don't know…" she started. She was so confused and did not know where to begin. She just now realized that this was not her burden. This was not her story and it was too heavy to carry. She consoled herself that it was for the best of everyone in the house but she looked around the room and saw sadness all over. She questioned all that she stood for.

"Look, it's okay you guys," Mark cut in. "Well, as you all know, after my accident last year, I needed blood and I discovered that my only match was mom. I had heard some rumors before about mom getting married to dad with me already born and if we follow their stories keenly, some of the mathematics of when I was born and when they met was not adding up. Besides, we can all agree that my features and dad's don't really match. Jabari and I decided to do a DNA test. We stole Dad's DNA- don't prosecute us- and the truth came out. I did not want to burden anyone with that information. As far as I am concerned, I was raised by a wonderful man, who I would not trade for anyone else, and I am forever grateful." He paused and looked at Ruthie, "Although I should have hired these detectives here if I wanted to know my roots. Ruthie, I know what you must be thinking, and I know you mean well, but ambushing us was really not your best idea. But since we are here, we might as well do this."

Jabari stepped in, "Mom, dad, we really appreciate you protecting us all these years and doing your absolute best to give us everything, but sooner or later you knew that this was coming. I'm sorry it had to be this way."

Ruthie was encouraged by what her brothers said. She looked at them with a lot of gratitude in her eyes. She knew they had her back and were trying to make it all better. "Ms. Amari, I apologize also for dragging in your innocent family into all this. I know that you want what is best for your family. Ethan loves you so much and I believe you are just protecting them. We have all made mistakes in the past and we are calling a truce. Please bear with us." Ethan's mother kept quiet and nodded, then shot a glance at Ruthie's parents, then down at her woven hands. "Do not be afraid, you all probably signed documents forbidding this conversation and since Ethan and I breached that, I believe its null and void since we were not party to it anyway. That must be a convincing argument in a court of law, right?" she asked looking at her dad and sisters and finally her mother, who just smiled and shook her head.

"Look who finally decided to practice some law despite denying it all these years," her mother talked for the first time since it all began, smiling. "Okay, let's just call it a truce and forget all the legal shenanigans just for the afternoon.

We might as well rip this bandage off and deal with the consequences," she added more seriously, creasing her brow as she avoided Ms. Vaughn's general area with her eyes. "We have made mistakes in the past, some due to fear and others for everyone's own protection, but I assure you, I never meant to hurt anyone, especially not you, baby girl. I couldn't help but blame myself after learning about what had happened to you was partly my fault. I am really sorry."

For the first time, Mrs. Chuma raised her glittery eyes towards Ms. Vaughn, she blinked and some tears fell freely down her cheeks. "Nora, we have been fighting for years and years, and I know I am the worst person you have ever met. I made your stay a living hell and I am truly sorry. I know I apologized before, but I was doing it with the legal documents in my hands and threats. I was so scared for Ruthie at that time and maybe I did not mean it. She really was affected after the lunch you had and we were scared she might fall into a depression. She had a rough childhood due to the decisions we made in our careers. I really am sorry, Jack, Derrick. I hope that one day you will find it in your hearts to forgive me."

"You are right, I have always detested you and frankly, I don't look forward to being friends with you. I still resent you. But in a way, you made me the strong woman I am now. I had to hustle from nothing, I lost my job when you sent me to that mental asylum, claiming that I was crazy for two whole months. Nelly here had to raise my boys, and that cemented our friendship. At least an amazing sister came out of all this. Ruthie, I know you mean well but maybe this is something you should have discussed with your family before calling us," Ms. Vaughn said. Everyone opened their eyes wide in astonishment at the mention of the asylum.

"We are all family here, and we need to lay everything down," Ruthie offered.

"Look, you abandoned us for more than twenty-five years, and our mother refusing your child maintenance was the best choice she made. We didn't need you then and we don't need you now. We have been great and all. Ethan man, we are sorry, and you can date Ruthie; she is an amazing lady and we loved her, we still do. We just don't think it's necessary to do all this and involve people not party to this. Do you expect us to join hands, sing *kumbaya*, and pretend that the past twenty-five years did not happen? I don't think so," Jack piped in.

Ruthie was getting frustrated now, one step forward and three back.

Derrick added, "Besides we are now talking about things that don't even concern us, like who fathered who; why is it relevant? Everyone chose who to raise and who to neglect and we have lived life with that arrangement." There was pain in his eyes as he said the last statement, looking directly into his biological father's eyes.

The room went silent. Ruthie felt like dismissing the whole thing and taking the first vehicle back to the city, but the milk was already spilt, she might as well bring in a cat to lick it all up. She sighed in frustration as everyone remained silent as if in deep thought. Betty took this as her cue to call in the waiter. She rose and went for the door. The waiter came in with a tray, picking up all the glasses as waiters brought in food that had been pre-ordered by Betty. There was steak and *ugali* while some asked for fries. Ms. Vaughn, the female twins, and Ruthie had the roasted chicken. Bottles of wine, some fresh juice for the minors, and beers for the men. The waiter left and came after a while with the drink orders. The whole time, everyone was mumbling in low tones. Ethan,

Betty, and Ruthie were strategizing on the way forward and seemed to be at a loss.

After the waiter had shut the doors, Mr. Chuma looked around the room and saw how distressed Ruthie was and cleared his throat. "Okay, I believe this whole situation calls for my communication. It is my fault, after all, and it is unfair to let little Ruthie deal with all this by herself. I would much rather tell the whole story, and I promise to try and tell the whole truth as I know it. You all hate me right now and you will be invited to respond. This is not a court, I am just a man who tried his best with my family and career. I did some shameful things that I regret." He started earning some eye rolls from the other side of the room. He took a tiny sip of his beer and continued, "My wife and I met in the course of our career; she had just moved to town and was raising Mark all by herself. She was strong willed and determined and I fell in love with her. I helped in raising Mark until she got pregnant with Jabari. I promised to be by her side and support her but she wasn't into marriage back then and was really afraid that I would leave, just like Mark's dad, despite my reassurance that I wouldn't. She refused marriage and I got so frustrated; that is when I met Norah. We became close friends and she was so civil about things and we had a good time until she got pregnant as well. After she gave birth, things became tough, and I told her that I was also raising two other boys. She fell into a depression and detested me. I tried my best to support her but I was at the peak of my career as a judge and my image mattered a lot to me at the time. I tried keeping things under wraps but Norah and I just could not agree on anything. She kept threatening to ruin my life and career and we had a horrible breakup."

"Nelly here stood by her and even tried calling lawyers on me and that was when I reconnected with Pamela.

She helped a lot. We fought them, resulting in Norah being institutionalized, and shamefully won. She drafted documents, forbidding them from ever coming forward with any more claims and we had to come up with a child maintenance agreement. Life was difficult. When Norah came out of the mental hospital, she was different. She joined hands with Nelly and started their businesses; she made the best out of her situation. As her sons grew, they stepped up and helped Norah. I was proud of them, deep down. I kept tabs on you for a few years and then I just stopped. I never stopped depositing money for the twins in an account and I was hoping that one day, one way or another, that they would get it, even if it was indirectly.

"Jack and Derrick, I know you loathe me, I would loathe me too. But I got you into Law School. That scholarship was to go to some other people and I had to put in a good word for you two. I am sorry for that as well.

"Mark, I'm sorry you had to find out about it all this way but I'm glad you took a slow play on it. We can talk about it back at home. Ruthie, going behind your back and threatening these people for my selfish gain was just plain evil of me. I am really sorry for everything I put all of you through. I am willing to work my debt around it and we can all start over.

"Please, let's just talk about this and try to come to an agreement for the sake of our children and keeping harmony in this family. I will not talk about this Ruthie-Ethan thing for now, though; we have a lot on our plate."

When he was done talking, everyone was quiet and Ruthie was dumbfounded. What was the next step? She wished she was a mind reader. Betty then spoke up, "I am the most irrelevant person here, I know, and we have been fed with a lot of things to chew on. We had come with documents and PowerPoint presentations, because we thought we needed them," she giggled and so did everyone else, "but, it seems we won't be needing them."

Betty continued, "Ms. Amari, you raised a fine young, strong man here and what he did for Ruthie in a span of the past three or four months is beyond what I have seen overtime. I give him a mark of approval and ask Ruthie, those are really rare for me to dish out. So please, give them a chance. We are not sure if it's love, but whatever they have is pure and genuine."

Ms. Amari nodded and smiled.

"Ethan, I know you heard what I said but if you break your promises I will pull off your arm and hit you with it. But as you can see I will only be the first in line. These two," she added, pointing at Mark and Jabari, "will be next. When they are done with you, we will be picking your beautiful beard at the shores of the River *Ndarugu*."

Everyone laughed.

"Well after that we will have him for dinner," Derrick added. "Seriously though, Ruthie is a fine young lady and we liked her when we spent time with her, salt of the earth. She is our half-sister and we appreciate her."

Relief flooded the room. Everyone smiled fondly at the twin brothers who were blushing now.

"We have no problem with Ruthie or her brothers and sisters. If she is anything to go by, then they are a bunch of wonderful people that we would like to know more. Mom was so attached to her before we all knew the truth and that says a lot," Jack said. "This hatred only goes so far as we allow it to; some of us have committed no crime. Maybe we should allow the grown-ups to deal with this at their level."

"I agree, son," started Nelly, Ethan's mother. "I had grown really fond of Ruthie, and your children seem nice and civil as well, but, like Betty, we are not party to this. Maybe we should allow the Chumas and Ms. Vaughn have this conversation. I will be there as well, Derrick, don't be worried. No documents, no signing anything. Just have the talk and come up with something palatable for all of us. This has gone on long enough and we need to let go and move on. Is that okay?" she said, looking around the room. Everyone nodded.

Betty rushed to the kitchen to delay their order by an hour and the children left the room. They went to the bar area and the boys played snooker while the ladies stayed close by, just catching up. They had fun getting to know each other and realized that they had a lot more in common than anticipated. Ruthie looked at Ethan longingly, appreciating the fact that this was a product of their relationship. How long was their relationship going to last? She wondered.

"Earth to Ruthie," Betty said, snapping her hands in front of Ruthie's eyes. "I have been calling you for the past thirty seconds while you were busy making googly eyes at Ethan. What do you think they are talking about?" Ruthie snapped from her daydream and just shrugged; she was hoping for the best.

Ms. Vaughn came out, her eyes red and teary and called them inside. They all went in, filled with tension. They found Ms. Amari and Pamela laughing at their private joke and everyone was relieved. After they had settled in, Ms. Vaughn started, "I know there has been a lot of bad blood in the past, but we have decided that we are going to put our differences aside for a moment and allow all of you to get to know each other and catch up. It is going to be very complicated at first but soon we will work out the dynamic. You can start by exchanging contacts and meeting up amongst yourselves at your own time, and we can also organize some time to be spending with each other during holidays."

She continued, "I know my sons will have a problem at first dealing with the whole paternity thing, but he will not expect the whole "father of the year" treatment. We will take baby steps and when we are all comfortable, we can include everyone."

They all nodded.

"Let's start on a clean slate then," she finished off as the waiter walked in with their meals. "We can all sit together and have a meal for a start. Don't let the pressure of all this affect your relationship, Ruthie and Ethan; this is just the beginning. We don't know what the future holds."

Ruthie and Ethan shared a look and blushed simultaneously. Then she whispered in his ear, "I can't believe we did this." He just smiled and focused on his food.

"Before I forget, Ethan, I hope our little exchange back at your house does not give you the idea that you can talk to us the way you want. That was the first and the last time, am I clear?"

"Yes sir, I truly apologize, emotions were high and that is the last time, I promise. I am sorry too, Mrs. Chuma," he responded giving a slight bow at the end.

"Don't worry about it. It's water under the bridge. Can we at least discuss how we will start with this blended-family issue?" replied Pamela.

"We could start by doing a friendly parental responsibility agreement, with favorable conditions for both-" started Mr. Chuma before he was cut off by Ms. Vaughn.

"You and your papers. I am not signing anything with you guys again. All these documents make my head spin and I feel like I am tied to something horrible. It gives me a lot of pressure. Why don't we start by burning all the agreements we have had over the years? It will make me feel free."

"You are absolutely right. Now that everything is on the table, let's start by having a ceremonial burning of the contracts at our backyard next weekend. We can have dinner and we will officially welcome you into our home," agreed Pamela.

"Yes, we will come for the ceremony of whatever you've called it, provided there is food and drinks," stated Jack as everyone laughed at the end.

"I hope Betty will be among the chefs, I have heard some good things about her cooking," said Derrick as he winked at Betty. She blushed as Ruthie beamed at her, making a mental note to tease her about it later on.

They decided to start off with that to mark the new beginning in their relationship. Mr. Chuma thought about how far they had come with this whole situation. He thought that it would end up much worse than it turned out. He looked at Ruthie and smiled to himself; she was stubborn but she was one great daughter.

"What about you, Mark? Are you going to trace your father and confront him?" asked Amani and Amina, each taking a question.

"Well, my situation is a bit different. I will have to talk to mom and dad about it first to know how we will proceed."

"As long as you still stay with us, we have no problem," said Amina.

"Don't worry kiddo, I'm not going anywhere."

They finished up their meals and continued drinking until it was dark. The waiter walked in with their bill and placed it in the middle of the table.

"So, Ruthie and Ethan, how did you plan to pay for this? We are your guests today," said Mr. Chuma. Ruthie and Ethan looked at each other wide-eyed.

"Yes, we were also invited here and I believe it's time to go. Thank you, children," Ms. Amari and Vaughn stood up with Ruthie's parents. Everyone pretended to gather their things ready to leave as Ruthie and Ethan looked at each other in fear; even Betty was in on the joke.

"Well, I'll be in the car guys," she said leaving the room.

"Guys, seriously, we were hoping we would all chip in on the bill, are you serious?" Ruthie started. Ethan just looked around with mixed feelings. *Was this a test? Are they serious?*

"Hurry up, we will be in the car," said Ruthie's mother as she left the room.

They all left the room and left Ruthie and Ethan still sat as they looked at the bill. "Do you think they will be coming back? How much can you pay right now?" they deliberated. They each looked at their accounts in their phone apps and they were still short altogether.

"Wait a minute, this bill is exaggerated, did we have all these?" said Ruthie as she went through the bill. "Nobody drank this expensive whiskey; who even had pork roast? Is this a whole pig? Where is the waiter?"

Suddenly, the door burst open and everyone burst in laughing.

"Serves you right for pulling this on all of us!" said Derrick.

"Whose brilliant idea was this? I can't believe you guys. Even you, Betty?" said Ruthie as she threw the fake bill on the table. Ethan was still seated with visible sweat on his forehead.

"It was all *Moi*" said Ms. Vaughn as she walked in the room with a dramatic cat walk, raising her arms above her head as she posed and smiled. She then rested them on her waist as everyone applauded. "Gotcha! Next time you will think twice before pulling a fast one on us. You totally deserved it."

They all laughed as Jack punched Ethan's arm. He recovered and laughed along with them as he shook his head. "Never do that again, I was so scared for a minute there."

They took turns and made fun of the pair. Ruthie was annoyed but it soon melted into pleasure; this was a sign of hope. If they could work together like this, then they could live together as a family. Their hard work had paid off.

Ruthie sat in her bed that night after sleep had refused to come once more- only this time, she was at peace. She looked to her side and saw Betty sleeping soundly, then smiled. She opened her curtains so that she could take a peek at the stars. The night sky was filled with stars and a bright half-moon. Clear, the weather outside seemed to agree with her general mood: it was calm, peaceful and content. She meditated on the day's events and thought about how badly it would have ended up had things taken a different direction.

She thought about her quest to find a perfect life, an all-round young lady checking the right boxes. She had resolved to turning to salvation after all her mental breakdowns and therapies which only seemed to provide a short fix. Their house girl had hinted to her that if she needed an eternal fix. She needed Jesus in her life; only God could save her. Ruthie eventually joined fellowships and her friend Betty would understand her and tag along as it seemed to help her. She actually had a better outlook in life and even her appearance changed, she looked brighter.

Ruthie had been so busy trying to chase perfection in comparison to her family and even other people. She realized that every other person she thought was perfect had their flaws, especially her own parents. She thought about how Ethan embraced his flaws and how each of those families were comfortable with what they had and took whatever life threw at them and made the best out of it. She looked at Betty. She had been blind all along. Betty was the definition of a fighter and a designer of her own life. She had been trying to teach her life lessons through her own way of living. Betty had helpe her throughout their friendship but she had been too blind and stubborn.

She went to her drawer and took out a brand-new notebook, branding it as her diary. She called it "Brand New Ruthie." On the inside of the covers, she wrote, *I am the designer of my own world. I am unique, beautiful, strong, and independent. I am human and may mess up sometimes, but it is how I pick myself up that matters. I will not chase perfection, but I will chase my own unique destiny. I deserve it.*

She then thought about how she was never bold enough to try out new things with the fear of failing and remembered a quote from her favorite movie, *A Cinderella Story*. She added a statement at the bottom. *"Never let the fear of striking out, keep you from playing the game."* She put the book back into her drawer and went back to bed smiling. She didn't bother drawing back her curtains. It felt better falling asleep looking into the clear night skies as she fantasized and meditated on how great her life had turned out.

www.ingramcontent.com/pod-product-compliance
Lightning Source LLC
Chambersburg PA
CBHW030752110726
47900CB00008B/2575